MURDER NEXT DOOR

Jim and Ginger Cozy Mysteries Book 1

Arthur Pearce

Copyright © 2024 Arthur Pearce

All rights reserved.

No part of this book may be reproduced, distributed, or transmitted in any form or by any means, including photocopying, recording, or other electronic or mechanical methods, without the prior written permission of the author, except in the case of brief quotations embodied in critical reviews and certain other noncommercial uses permitted by copyright law. For permission requests, please contact the author.

"Murder Next Door" is a work of fiction. Names, characters, businesses, places, events and incidents either are products of the author's imagination or are used fictitiously. Any resemblance to actual persons, living or dead, events, or locales is entirely coincidental.

ISBN: 979-8-3413-2860-0

To my Ginger

Contents

Chapter 1	1
Chapter 2	15
Chapter 3	29
Chapter 4	37
Chapter 5	49
Chapter 6	63
Chapter 7	71
Chapter 8	83
Chapter 9	89
Chapter 10	101
Chapter 11	115
Chapter 12	127
Chapter 13	143
Chapter 14	153

Chapter 15	165
Chapter 16	173
Chapter 17	185
Chapter 18	201
Chapter 19	211
Chapter 20	223
Jim and Ginger's Next Case	233
Bonus Content	235

Chapter 1

My chin slipped off my hand as I caught myself nodding off again. I blinked rapidly, trying to focus on the computer screen in front of me. The library's new catalog system glared back, its interface as incomprehensible as ancient hieroglyphics. A glance at the wall clock told me there were still three more hours until closing time. I could do this.

"Mr. Butterfield?"

I jerked upright, nearly knocking over my mug of lukewarm coffee. Mrs. Higgins, the library manager, loomed over me, her lips pressed into a thin line.

"Yes, Mrs. Higgins?" I offered what I hoped was a charming smile.

She sighed. "Were you sleeping again?"

"No," I lied, straightening my tie. "Just... concentrating. This new system is quite complex, you know."

Mrs. Higgins' frown deepened. "It's been three months since we implemented it, Mr. Butterfield. Everyone else has adapted."

I nodded, trying not to yawn. It wasn't my fault technology seemed to advance at the speed of light these days.

Take last week, for instance. A young woman with thick-rimmed glasses had approached my desk. "Excuse me, where can I find books on gardening?"

"Ah, gardening! We have plenty of those books," I'd said, rising from my chair. "Follow me, I'll show you right to them."

I'd led her confidently through the stacks, muscle memory guiding my steps. We'd rounded the corner to where the gardening section had been for the past thirty years, only to find ourselves face-to-face with a wall of cookbooks.

"That's odd," I'd muttered, scratching my head. "They should be right here..."

The young woman had cleared her throat. "Um, actually, I just checked the library app. It says gardening is on the second floor now."

I'd felt my face flush. "Oh, right! They must have moved it. The second floor it is, then!"

Mrs. Higgins' voice snapped me back to the present. "Mr. Butterfield, are you listening to me?"

"Of course," I said, trying to focus on her face. She looked tired, the lines around her eyes more pronounced than usual.

"I was saying that we've had several complaints about you giving incorrect information to patrons. And now I find you asleep at the desk again." She shook her head. "This can't continue."

I straightened in my chair. "Mrs. Higgins, I assure you I'm fully committed to my work here. Perhaps I just need a refresher course on the new systems?"

She pinched the bridge of her nose. "We've already sent you to three training sessions, Jim. Three."

Had it really been that many? They all blurred together in a haze of confusing jargon and click-this, swipe-that instructions.

"Well, maybe fourth time's the charm?" I offered with hope in my voice.

Mrs. Higgins opened her mouth to reply, but was interrupted by a hesitant voice.

"Excuse me?" We both turned to see a middle-aged man holding a tattered paperback. "I was wondering if you had any more books by this author?"

"Certainly!" I said, grateful for the distraction. I looked at the book's cover. "Ah, Ruth Rendell. Excellent taste, sir. We have a whole section dedicated to mystery novels. Right this way!"

I stood, my knees creaking in protest, and led the man towards the fiction section. Or at least, where I thought the fiction section still was. We wandered through the stacks, passing history, biography, and what looked like a new area filled with computers.

"It should be right around here..." I muttered to myself.

"Mr. Butterfield." Mrs. Higgins' voice made me jump. She'd followed us, her expression a mix of exasperation and pity. "The mystery section is now on the east wall, remember? We moved it last month during the renovation."

"Oh, right!" I said, plastering on a smile. "Silly me. This way, sir!"

I could feel Mrs. Higgins' gaze behind my back as I led the man to the correct shelves. Once he was happily browsing, I turned to face my manager, anticipating another lecture.

But Mrs. Higgins just shook her head. "My office. Now."

My stomach sank as I followed her through the library. We passed the children's section, where a young librarian was reading a fairy tale to kids. I remembered when that had been my favorite part of the job, bringing books to life for wide-eyed little ones. Now, even the picture books had those bizarre square codes you were supposed to scan with your phone. Progress, they called it.

Mrs. Higgins closed her office door behind us and gestured for me to sit in one of the chairs facing her desk. Once settled into her own seat, she exhaled a weary sigh.

"Jim," she began, her tone gentler than I'd expected. "You've been with this library for over forty years. Your dedication to books and to our patrons has always been unquestionable."

I nodded, a lump forming in my throat. I knew where this was going.

"But the world is changing," she continued. "Libraries aren't just about books anymore. We're community centers, technology hubs. We need to adapt to serve our patrons better."

"I understand that," I said, my voice rough. "And I'm trying, I really am."

Mrs. Higgins gave me a sad smile. "I know you are. But it's not enough. We can't have staff members falling asleep at the desk or giving patrons outdated information. It's not fair to them, and it's not fair to your colleagues who have to pick up the slack."

I slumped in my chair, feeling every one of my sixty-eight years. "So this is it, then? You're firing me?"

She winced at my bluntness. "I'm afraid we don't have much choice. But you'll always be welcome here as a patron."

I nodded numbly, barely hearing anything she rattled off about severance and benefits. My mind drifted to happier times, when the library had been my second home. Happier, pre-Internet times.

"Jim? Jim, are you listening?"

I blinked, focusing on Mrs. Higgins' concerned face. "Sorry, just... remembering."

She nodded sympathetically. "Why don't you take the rest of the day to process this? Come in tomorrow to clean out your desk and say your goodbyes."

I stood on shaky legs, feeling like I'd aged another decade in the past hour. "Right. Thank you, Mrs. Higgins."

I turned to leave, but her voice stopped me at the door. "For what it's worth, Jim, I really am sorry it's come to this."

I managed a weak smile. "Me too."

I shuffled back to my desk, my mind whirling with thoughts of what I was supposed to do now. The library had been my life for so long. I slumped into my chair, barely noticing as I jostled my forgotten mug of coffee.

Time seemed to slow as I watched the mug tip, its contents arcing through the air in slow motion. I stared in horror as the lukewarm liquid splashed across my keyboard and screen which flickered, and then went dark. In that moment, I knew my fate was sealed. There would be no chance of appealing Mrs. Higgins' decision.

As if summoned by my catastrophic clumsiness, Mrs. Higgins appeared at my side. She took in the scene – the ruined computer, my shocked expression – and let out a long, slow breath.

"Oh, Jim," she said, her voice a mix of sympathy and resignation. "I think perhaps it's best if you go home now. We'll sort out the rest tomorrow."

I nodded silently, gathering my things with trembling hands. As I walked towards the exit, I could feel the eyes of my colleagues on my back. Some looked confused, others pitying.

The automatic doors opened, and I stepped out into the bright afternoon sun. It felt wrong somehow, that the world could look so cheerful when mine had just fallen apart. I stood on the library steps, blinking in the light, and wondered what on earth I was going to do next.

***

I trudged up the three flights of stairs to my apartment, each step feeling heavier than the last. The key stuck in the lock, as it always did, requiring a bit of jiggling before the door finally creaked open. I stepped into the dim hallway, not bothering to turn on the lights.

The apartment smelled musty, a mix of old books and neglect. I'd never been much for housekeeping, and without Martha around to gently prod me, things had gotten a bit... dusty. I sneezed as I shrugged off my coat, sending a small cloud of particles dancing in the fading afternoon light that filtered through the grimy windows.

"Home sweet home," I muttered to no one in particular.

I went to the living room, navigating around stacks of books that had long ago outgrown my overstuffed shelves. I sank into the familiar embrace of my armchair with a groan.

For a long moment, I just sat there, staring at the blank TV screen. The events of the day played on repeat in my mind – Mrs. Higgins' disappointed frown, the coffee spilling across the keyboard, the pitying looks from my coworkers. My chest tightened. Forty-three years at the library, gone in an afternoon.

"Well," I said, my voice sounding too loud in the quiet apartment, "I suppose I could use a change of clothes."

I heaved myself out of the chair and made my way to the bedroom. The wardrobe door stuck, as usual, requiring a firm yank to open. As I reached for a fresh shirt, my hand brushed against something soft and familiar. I paused, and then slowly pulled out the lumpy, hand-knitted sweater.

Martha had made it for me, that must have been fifteen years ago now. The yarn was a horrendous shade of mustard yellow – she'd always had unique taste in colors. I held it up, chuckling at the uneven stitches and the slightly lopsided collar.

"You always did say it was the thought that counted, my dear," I murmured, running my thumb over a small hole near the cuff.

The chuckling died in my throat as a wave of grief washed over me. One year. One year since I'd lost her, and some days it still felt like yesterday.

I sank onto the edge of the bed, clutching the sweater to my chest. Martha's face swam before my eyes – not as she'd looked near the end, gaunt and pale in her hospital bed, but vibrant and full of life, her eyes twinkling with mischief.

"You're brooding again, old man," I could almost hear her say. "What did I tell you about that?"

I smiled despite myself. "That it makes me look like a constipated bulldog," I replied to the empty room.

Martha had never been one to mince words. Even when the doctors had given her the diagnosis – stage four lung cancer, inoperable – she'd just nodded and said, "Well, I suppose that's what I get for smoking like a chimney all these years."

I'd tried to argue, to say it wasn't her fault, but she'd just waved me off. "No use crying over spilled milk, Jimmy," she'd said. "Or tar-filled lungs in my case."

That was my Martha – facing down even death with a wry smile and a terrible joke.

I clutched the sweater tighter, breathing in deeply. If I concentrated hard enough, I could almost catch a smell of her perfume – a cheap brand she'd worn for decades, claiming it was "good enough for government work."

My eyes drifted to the framed photo on the nightstand. It was from our 30th anniversary trip to the coast. We're standing on a rocky beach, the ocean behind us. Martha's gray hair is whipping around her face in the wind, and she's grinning like a schoolgirl. I'm next to her, looking slightly uncomfortable as always when faced with a camera.

"Remember what you said that day?" I asked the Martha in the photo. "About Oceanview Cove?"

We'd driven through some little seaside town on our way home. Martha had practically pressed her nose to the car window, enjoying the sight of the quaint shops and colorful houses.

"Oh, Jim," she'd sighed, a dreamy look in her eyes. "It reminds me of my hometown, Oceanview Cove. You know, that would be a perfect place for us to retire. Just imagine..."

I'd laughed, interrupting her. "What, leave the city for some tiny fishing village?"

But Martha had been serious. "Why not? That's where I grew up. And my parents said they would leave me their house nestled on the hillside overlooking the ocean. We could live there, spend our golden years watching the waves roll in."

I'd hummed noncommittally, focused on navigating the winding coastal road. But Martha had been relentless, telling me about lazy mornings and sunset walks on the beach. By the time we'd returned home, I'd found myself actually considering the idea.

Of course, life had a way of getting in the way. There was always another reason to put it off – work was too busy, the grandkids were starting school, the basement needed cleaning out. And then... well, then it was too late.

I set the sweater aside and stood. "No time like the present, I suppose," I muttered, pulling an old suitcase from under the bed.

I moved through the apartment with newfound purpose, gathering clothes and toiletries. My collection of mystery novels posed a challenge – how to choose which ones to bring? In the end, I settled on a mix of old favorites and ones I hadn't gotten around to reading yet.

As I packed, I found myself talking to Martha, as I often did when alone in the apartment.

"You'll be pleased to know I'm finally taking your advice, my dear," I said, methodically folding shirts and placing them in the suitcase. "Though I suppose being forcibly retired wasn't quite what you had in mind."

I could almost hear her laugh. "Better late than never, Jimmy. You always did need a kick in the pants to get moving."

I paused in my packing, a thought suddenly occurring to me. I should call Sarah and let her know what's happening.

I pulled my ancient flip phone out of my pocket, squinting at the tiny screen as I scrolled through the contacts. Our daughter picked up on the third ring.

"Dad? Is everything okay?" Sarah's voice was tinged with concern. I didn't usually call in the middle of the day.

"Everything's fine, sweetheart," I assured her. "Well, mostly fine. I've had a bit of a... career change."

"A career change?" She sounded skeptical. "Dad, you've worked at the library since before I was born."

I chuckled. "Yes, well, it seems the library and I have decided to part ways. Creative differences, you might say."

"Oh, Dad." Sarah's voice softened. "I'm so sorry. Are you alright?"

"I'm... adjusting," I said, surprising myself with how true it felt. "Actually, I've decided to make a bit of a life change. I'm moving to Oceanview Cove."

There was a long pause. "Oceanview Cove? Isn't that where Mom..."

"Where your mother grew up, yes," I finished. "She always wanted us to retire there, remember? Seems like a good time to fulfill that dream."

"But Dad, that's hours away! What about your life in the city? What about us?"

I sighed. "Sarah, honey, you live in Nashville, which is already hours away from me. It's not like I see you and the kids every week as it is. And as for the rest... well, sometimes a man needs a fresh start."

Another pause. When Sarah spoke again, her voice was calmer. "You're sure about this?"

"I am," I said, surprising myself with how confident I felt. "Your mother left us that house nestled on the hillside overlooking the ocean. It's about time someone made use of it."

"Okay," Sarah said slowly. "If you're sure. But promise me you'll call if you need anything. And we'll come visit as soon as we can."

"Of course, sweetheart. Give my love to Tom and the kids."

After we hung up, I stood in the middle of the cluttered living room, surveying the life I was preparing to leave behind. It was strange how forty years could be condensed into a couple of suitcases and a box of books.

My eyes fell on the mantelpiece, where a collection of framed photos stood. I walked over and picked up my favorite – Martha and me on our wedding day. We were so young, so full of hope for the future. I traced Martha's smiling face with my finger, carefully wrapped the photo in a sweater, and then tucked it into my suitcase.

I spent the next day sorting out things at the library. Mrs. Higgins, to her credit, had been true to her word about the benefits. It wasn't much, but combined with my savings and pension, it would be enough to live on comfortably in Oceanview Cove. I said my goodbyes to my colleagues, some of whom I'd known for decades, and went out of the library one last time.

With the loose ends tied up, I found myself on a sunny Tuesday morning, loading the last of my bags into my old Buick LeSabre. The car groaned in protest as I slammed the trunk shut.

I climbed into the driver's seat and took one last look at the apartment building that had been my home for so many years. It looked smaller somehow, less significant now that I was leaving it behind.

"Well, my dear," I said softly, imagining Martha in the empty passenger seat, "I hope you're ready for one last ride."

The city streets rolled by outside the window, familiar sights already beginning to feel like memories. But for once, I didn't look back. My gaze was fixed firmly ahead, towards the horizon and whatever waited for me in Oceanview Cove.

It was a long drive to the coast, but I had time. All the time in the world, really. And as the cityscape faded in my rearview mirror, replaced by rolling countryside, I felt a weight lifting from my shoulders.

This was it. A new chapter. A fresh start. And who knew? Maybe there were still a few surprises left in store for the old librarian after all.

Chapter 2

I stopped my old Buick on a sun-dappled street, just outside Martha's house. For a moment, I just sat there, hands gripping the steering wheel, staring at the scene before me.

Oceanview Cove spread out like a picture postcard, all pastel-colored cottages and weathered fishing boats bobbing in the harbor. The setting sun painted the sky in shades of pink and gold, reflecting off windows and casting long shadows across neatly trimmed lawns. It was, I had to admit, breathtaking.

I took a deep breath and opened the car door. The salty air hit me like a slap, bringing with it the cries of seagulls and the distant crash of waves. As I stretched, working out the kinks from the long drive, I noticed something... odd. The town was quiet. Too quiet. Where were the sounds of children playing, of neighbors chatting, of life being lived? The only movement I could see was a stray cat slinking between two houses, its eyes glinting in the fading light.

"Charming," I muttered, suppressing a shiver that had nothing to do with the cool evening breeze.

I popped the trunk and began unloading my luggage. By the time I'd wrestled the last suitcase onto the sidewalk, I was puffing like a steam engine.

The old house with peeling blue paint and a wraparound porch loomed before me. Martha's childhood home. Our retirement dream.

I inserted the key, fumbling with the unfamiliar lock. The door creaked open, revealing a musty interior that smelled of sea air.

"Home sweet home," I sighed, dragging my suitcases over the threshold.

The house was like stepping back in time. Faded floral wallpaper, dust on every surface, and enough knick-knacks to stock a small antique shop. Martha's parents had clearly been collectors – or perhaps just incapable of throwing anything away.

I made my way to the bedroom. The bed was made up with the quilt that looked older than I was, but at least it seemed clean. I sank onto it gratefully, my back resting after the long car ride.

As I sat there, the reality of my situation began to sink in. Here I was, a 68-year-old widower, starting over in a small town where I knew no one. What on earth had I been thinking?

I pulled my phone out of my pocket, squinting at the screen. No signal. Of course.

Grumbling, I began wandering the house, holding my phone aloft like some sort of technological divining rod. I finally found a bar of signal in the kitchen, standing on my tiptoes next to the window.

Sarah picked up on the second ring. "Dad? Are you there? How was the drive?"

"I'm here," I said, trying to keep the weariness out of my voice. "The drive was fine. Long, but fine."

"And the house? Is it... livable?"

I glanced around the kitchen, taking in the ancient appliances and the wallpaper that might have been cheerful sometime during the Nixon administration.

"It's... quaint," I settled on. "Needs a bit of work, but it's got potential."

Sarah's sigh of relief was audible even through the spotty connection. "That's great, Dad. I was worried it might be falling apart after all these years."

"Oh, it's standing firm," I assured her. "Like a..." I searched for an appropriate comparison. "Like a very old, slightly crooked tree."

Sarah laughed, the sound warming me more than I thought it would. "Well, I'm glad you made it safely. Are you sure you're going to be okay there? All alone?"

"I'll be fine," I said, more confidently than I felt. "Your mother always said this town was full of friendly people. I'm sure I'll be making friends in no time."

There was a pause on the other end of the line. When Sarah spoke again, her voice was softer. "I'm proud of you, Dad. For doing this. For living Mom's dream."

I swallowed hard, blinking away the sudden moisture in my eyes. "Yes, well. Better late than never, I suppose."

We chatted for a few more minutes, and as I hung up, I realized the kitchen had grown dark, the last of the sunlight fading from the sky. I turned a light switch on, wincing as harsh fluorescent light flooded the room. In the sudden brightness, something caught my eye outside the window. A figure, standing at the edge of my property, staring at the house.

I blinked, and it was gone.

"Get a grip, old man," I muttered, rubbing my eyes. "You're letting your imagination run wild."

I chuckled to myself, the sound echoing in the empty room. Welcome to Oceanview Cove, I thought. Let the thrilling life of a retiree begin.

***

I woke the next morning to the unfamiliar sound of seagulls squabbling outside my window. For a moment, I lay there disoriented, wondering where on earth I was. Then it all came rushing back – the move, the house, Oceanview Cove.

"Right," I muttered, hauling myself out of bed. "New life begins today, Jim."

After a quick shower in the ancient bathroom I made my way downstairs. The kitchen looked less depressing in the morning light, but the empty cupboards reminded me that I needed to do some serious grocery shopping.

"Coffee first," I decided, rummaging through my bags until I found the jar of instant I'd brought from home. It wasn't ground coffee, but it would do the job.

As the kettle boiled, I peered out the windows at my new neighborhood. The street was still quiet, but I could see signs of life stirring – curtains being drawn back, a newspaper delivery boy on a bicycle.

I took my coffee out to the porch, settling into a weathered rocking chair. The wood creaked ominously under my weight, but held. The air was crisp and salty, carrying the faint scent of the sea. It was peaceful, a stark contrast to the constant bustle of the city.

After finishing my coffee, I decided it was time to tackle the rest of my unpacking. Last night I was too exhausted from the drive to do more than stumble into bed.

I was in the midst of moving my suitcases from the car when I heard a cheerful voice call out, "Need a hand there, neighbor?"

I turned to see a man about my age striding across the lawn. He was tall and lean, with a full head of silver hair and a smile so bright it could've lit up the whole street.

"Oh, I wouldn't want to trouble you," I started to say, but he was already reaching for one of my bags.

"Nonsense," he said, easily lifting a suitcase I'd been struggling with. "What are neighbors for? I'm Peter, by the way. Peter Johnson. Live right next door."

"Jim Butterfield," I replied, following him up the porch steps. "Just moved in yesterday."

Peter set the suitcase down in the hallway and turned to me with a grin. "Well, Jim Butterfield, welcome to Oceanview Cove. How are you finding it so far?"

I hesitated, not wanting to offend my new neighbor by mentioning the eerie quiet or the strange figure I'd glimpsed last night. "It's... quaint," I settled on. "Quite a change from the city."

Peter laughed. "Oh, I bet. But you'll get used to the pace of life here. This town grows on you." He glanced at his watch. "I'm having a few beers this evening. Why don't you join me? Get to know each other properly."

The offer caught me off guard. It had been a long time since I'd socialized with anyone outside of work. But then, wasn't that the whole point of this move? To start fresh, maybe make some friends?

"That sounds great," I heard myself saying. "What time?"

"Let's say around seven? Just come on over whenever you're ready." Peter started heading back to his house. "And Jim? Don't worry about bringing anything. Consider it a welcome to the neighborhood gift."

I watched him go, feeling a mix of anticipation and nerves. A beer with the neighbor. It was a start, at least.

I'd just turned back to my unpacking when another voice called out, "Yoo-hoo! New neighbor!"

I sighed. So much for the quiet town.

A portly man with thinning hair and round, wire-rimmed glasses was hurrying across the street towards me. He had the eager look of someone who'd just discovered a fresh source of gossip.

"Ryan Perkins," he announced, thrusting out a hand as he reached me. "Neighborhood watch captain and editor of the Oceanview Cove Gazette. Small paper, but we keep the town informed!"

I shook his hand, trying not to wince at his enthusiastic grip. "Jim Butterfield. Nice to meet you."

"Butterfield, Butterfield," Ryan mused, tapping his chin. "Any relation to the Parkers? This was their old place, wasn't it?"

"My late wife, Martha," I explained. "She grew up here and inherited the house from her parents."

Ryan's eyes lit up. "Martha Parker! Of course, I remember her. Lovely girl, always had her nose in a book. Left town right after high school, if I recall correctly. So sorry about her passing. My condolences."

I nodded, unsure how to respond to this flood of information about my wife's past.

Ryan didn't seem to notice my discomfort. He continued, "So, Jim, tell me all about yourself! What brings you to our little paradise? Retiring, are you? What did you do before? Any hobbies? Kids?"

The questions came rapid-fire, leaving me feeling a bit overwhelmed. "I, uh... yes, retiring. I was a librarian. One daughter, two grandkids. And I... read, I suppose?"

Ryan nodded eagerly at each piece of information, as if I was sharing earth-shattering news. "Fascinating, fascinating. A librarian! You must have so many stories. We should sit down for a proper interview sometime. For the Gazette, you know."

"Right," I said weakly. "That sounds... great."

Ryan opened his mouth, no doubt to launch into another bunch of questions, but I cut him off. "Actually, Ryan, I was wondering – is there anything special I should know about the town? Any local attractions?"

It was a desperate attempt to change the subject, but it worked. Ryan's face lit up. "Oh, where to begin! Oceanview Cove is simply brimming with charm and history. Did you know we were founded in 1823 by a group of..."

I let Ryan's words wash over me, nodding at appropriate intervals. He seemed to have an encyclopedic knowledge of the town's history, peppered with gossip about various residents both past and present.

"...and of course, there's Maggie's Bakery," Ryan was saying as I tuned back in. "Best croissants in the world. You simply must try them."

"Maggie's Bakery," I repeated, seizing on this piece of actually useful information. "I'll have to check it out."

Ryan nodded enthusiastically. "Oh, you won't regret it. Maggie's been running that place for almost twenty years now. Sweetest lady you'll ever meet."

I made a mental note to visit the bakery. It would at least save me from having to figure out the ancient oven in the kitchen.

Ryan glanced at his watch and let out a theatrical gasp. "Oh my, I've got to run, Jim. Paper doesn't put itself together." He started walking towards his house, still talking. "But we'll catch up soon, so much more to discuss! Welcome to Oceanview Cove!"

I watched him hurry off, feeling a bit like I'd just been through a hurricane. Was everyone in this town so enthusiastic?

Shaking my head, I turned back to my unpacking. The rest of the morning passed in a blur of arranging and rearranging, trying to make this space feel like home. I hung my clothes in the musty wardrobe, placed my books on the sagging shelves, and carefully arranged the few photos I'd brought on the mantelpiece.

As I worked, I couldn't help but imagine Martha here as a young girl, running up and down the creaky stairs, sitting in the chair on the porch with a book on summer afternoons. It was strange, being surrounded by her childhood memories.

By mid-afternoon, I'd done all I could without buying new furniture or making major renovations. My stomach growled, reminding me that I still needed to stock the kitchen. But first things first – I had to try those famous Maggie's croissants.

I locked up the house and set off down the street, trying to remember the directions Ryan had rattled off. The town was livelier now, with people going about their daily business. A few nodded or waved as I passed, looking at me curiously. I rounded the corner and saw the cheerful sign for Maggie's Bakery ahead. Well, it wasn't half as far from my house as I'd expected, and easier to find than trying to locate my reading glasses on a cluttered desk.

I ambled along the narrow, cobblestone path toward the bakery, the scent of saltwater mingled with the aroma of freshly baked bread. My stomach growled in anticipation. Maybe this quaint little town had its perks after all.

The morning mist hadn't fully lifted, creating a mysterious atmosphere in the town. Colorful shopfronts loomed out of the haze, their cheery facades at odds with the chilly morning. I quickened my pace, suddenly eager for the warmth of the bakery.

"Well, well, well," a voice croaked from the fog. "What have we here?"

I nearly jumped out of my skin. Peering through the mist, I made out a figure emerging from between two buildings. As it drew closer, I realized it was a woman. She was draped in layers of colorful scarves, each one more vibrant than the other. Bangles jangled on her wrists, and around her neck hung an assortment of pendants and crystals that clinked together as she moved. Her silver hair was sticking out in all directions as if she'd just been electrocuted.

"Good morning," I said, trying to edge around her.

"Oh, it's a morning indeed," she cackled, looking at me with a piercing stare. "But whether it's good remains to be seen, doesn't it?"

I blinked, taken aback. "I'm sorry, do I know you?"

She laughed again, the sound echoing oddly in the misty street. "Know me? Oh, I should think not. But I know you, Jim Butterfield."

A chill ran down my spine. "How did you-"

"The stars, my dear. They whisper all sorts of secrets, if you know how to listen." She tapped the side of her nose conspiratorially. "I'm Emma, by the way. The one and only astrologer in the town."

"Ah," I said, not sure how else to respond. I glanced longingly toward the bakery, now visible through the thinning mist. "Well, it's been... interesting meeting you, Emma. But I really should be-"

"Not so fast," Emma said, her tone suddenly serious. She grabbed my arm with surprising strength, her bangles jangling. "The stars have a message for you, Jim Butterfield. And it's not one to be ignored."

I tried to pull away, but her grip was like iron. "Really, I don't think-"

"Danger," she hissed, her eyes wide behind her thick glasses. "I see danger in your near future. Dark clouds gathering on your horizon."

"That's just the sea mist," I said weakly, still trying to extricate myself.

Emma shook her head. "No, no, no. This is serious, Jim. The alignment of Jupiter with Mars... it's a bad omen. Very bad indeed."

I finally managed to free my arm, taking a step back. "Look, I appreciate the... warning. But I really don't believe in all this astrology business."

"Belief has nothing to do with it," Emma said. "The stars don't care if you believe in them or not. They speak the truth regardless."

She reached into one of her many pockets and pulled out a small, cloth-wrapped bundle. "Here," she said, giving it to me. "Take this. For protection."

Against my better judgment, I accepted the package. It was surprisingly heavy for its size. "What is it?"

"A lodestone," Emma said, as if that explained everything. "Keep it with you. It'll help ward off the darkness that's coming."

I stared at the bundle in my hand, then back at Emma. She met my gaze unflinchingly, her expression deadly serious.

"Right," I said slowly. "Well, thank you. I'll just... keep this safe then."

Emma nodded, apparently satisfied. "See that you do. And Jim?"

I paused in the act of pocketing the strange gift. "Yes?"

"Don't disregard what I said earlier. Watch your back in the next days." With that cryptic warning, she turned and melted back into the mist, her scarves fluttering behind her like exotic birds.

I stood there for a moment, the lodestone heavy in my pocket, trying to process what had just happened. Part of me wanted to dismiss Emma as a harmless eccentric, the kind of quirky character you'd expect to find in a small town.

But another part, a part I wasn't entirely comfortable acknowledging, felt unsettled. There had been something in her eyes, a certainty that went beyond mere play-acting. And how had she known my name?

The cheerful ding of a bell snapped me out of my thoughts. I looked up to see a young couple exiting the bakery, paper bag in hand. The smell of fresh pastries wafted toward me, momentarily dispelling the odd mood that had settled over me.

"Get a grip, Jim," I muttered to myself. "You're here for a new start, not to get caught up in some fortune-teller's fantasies."

Still, as I pushed open the door to Maggie's Bakery, I couldn't quite shake the feeling that Emma's warning had been more than just the ramblings of a local eccentric. The lodestone seemed to pulse in my pocket, a tangible reminder of her ominous predictions.

I had a feeling my retirement was going to be anything but quiet.

Chapter 3

I pushed open the door to Maggie's Bakery, and a wave of warm, fragrant air enveloped me. The rich scent of fresh bread and sugary pastries made my mouth water instantly. It was a stark contrast to the cool, salty breeze outside, like stepping into a different world entirely.

The bakery was bustling with activity. A line of customers stretched from the counter to the door, their soft chatter mingling with the clink of plates and the hiss of the espresso machine. Despite the crowd, there was a cozy, almost intimate atmosphere to the place.

I joined the queue, taking in my surroundings. The walls were a cheery yellow, adorned with vintage baking advertisements and black-and-white photos of the town. Wooden tables and chairs were scattered around the room, most occupied by locals enjoying their morning treats.

Behind the counter, a slightly plump, middle-aged woman wearing a flour-dusted apron worked tirelessly, her movements quick and practiced. She greeted each customer by name, her smile never faltering despite the morning rush. This had to be Maggie.

As the line moved forward, I found myself oddly nervous. It had been a long time since I'd had to introduce myself to a woman. In the library, my female colleagues had known me for years. Here, I was a stranger.

Finally, it was my turn. Maggie looked up, her warm brown eyes crinkling at the corners as she smiled. "Hello there! I don't believe we've met, you must be new here. I'm Maggie Brown."

I nodded. "Pleasure to meet you, Maggie! That's right, I'm new here. Jim Butterfield. I just moved into the old Parkers' place."

Maggie's eyes widened in recognition. "Oh, Martha Parker's husband! We've been wondering if you might ever come to our town. Martha was such a dear girl. I was so sorry to hear of her passing."

A lump formed in my throat. Even here, in this cheerful bakery, I couldn't escape the reminders of my loss. "Thank you," I managed. "She always spoke fondly of this town."

Maggie nodded sympathetically. "If you don't mind me asking, Jim, what made you decide to move to Oceanview Cove?"

I hesitated for a moment before replying. "Well, it was Martha's dream, actually. We always talked about retiring here, in her childhood home. After she passed... well, I thought it was time to fulfill that dream for her."

Maggie's eyes softened. "Oh, that's beautiful. Martha would be so pleased. And we're glad to have you here." She paused, then added with a gentle smile, "Now, what can

I get for you today? Might I recommend our croissants? They're something of a local legend, some people say."

Grateful for the change of subject, I ordered half a dozen croissants and a coffee. As Maggie bustled about, preparing my order, she kept up a steady stream of friendly chatter.

"So, Jim, how are you finding Oceanview Cove so far? Quite a change from the city, I imagine."

I chuckled. "It certainly is. Everyone seems to know everything about everyone else around here."

Maggie laughed, a warm, rich sound. "That's small-town life for you. No secrets in Oceanview Cove, that's for sure. But don't you worry, we take care of our own here."

As she handed me my bag of croissants, her expression turned serious. "Jim? If you need anything – anything at all – you just come see me, you hear? We all know how hard it can be, starting over."

I was touched by her kindness. "Thank you, Maggie. I appreciate that."

She waved off my thanks with a flour-covered hand. "Think nothing of it. Now, you enjoy those croissants. And don't be a stranger!"

I made my way to a small table by the window, holding my coffee and the warm bag of pastries. The first bite of croissant was heavenly – buttery, flaky, and still warm from the oven. Ryan hadn't been exaggerating; these might indeed rival any I'd had in my life.

As I savored my breakfast, I watched the comings and goings of the bakery. Maggie seemed to have a kind word for everyone, from the anxious mother with three small children to the gruff fisherman who barely grunted his order. She handled them all with the same cheerful efficiency.

I was so engrossed in people-watching that I almost didn't notice when someone slid into the chair across from me.

"So, what do you think of our Maggie?" Ryan's eager voice made me jump. "Best baker in the country, wouldn't you say?"

I blinked, thrown off balance by his sudden appearance. "Oh, yes. The croissants are excellent, the best I've ever had I would say." Then, remembering our earlier conversation, I added, "I thought you were heading to work on the paper?"

Ryan grinned. "Ah, well, I decided I needed a bit of fuel before diving into the day's news. And I couldn't pass up the chance to tell you more about this place." He leaned in conspiratorially. "You know, there's quite a story behind this bakery. Would you believe it used to be-"

"Ryan!" Maggie's voice cut through his whisper. "Are you bothering our new neighbor already?"

Ryan straightened up, looking like a schoolboy caught passing notes. "Just welcoming him to the community, Maggie dear."

Maggie shook her head fondly as she approached our table. "Don't let him talk your ear off, Jim. Ryan here fancies himself the town historian."

"Someone's got to keep the stories alive," Ryan protested good-naturedly.

"Mhmm," Maggie hummed, unconvinced. "And I'm sure it has nothing to do with digging up gossip for that newspaper of yours." She turned to me with a wink. "You watch out for this one, Jim. He'll have your life story on the front page before you can blink."

I chuckled, amused by their banter. It was clear there was real affection beneath the teasing. "I'll keep that in mind."

As Maggie returned to the counter, Ryan launched into a detailed history of the bakery building, complete with tales of prohibition-era smuggling and secret passages. I listened with half an ear, more interested in observing the dynamics of the place.

Everyone who came through the door seemed to know everyone else. They called out greetings, shared news, arranged meetups. It was like watching a well-choreographed dance, and I was acutely aware of my status as an outsider.

Eventually, Ryan's monologue wound down, and he excused himself to "make the rounds." I hastily finished my coffee, wiping a stray croissant crumb from my chin with my handkerchief before gathering my things to leave. While Ryan was engrossed in conversation with another patron, I seized the opportunity to make my exit, feeling a bit overwhelmed by the wealth of local history. As I stood, Maggie caught my eye from behind the counter and gave me a warm smile and a little wave.

I pushed open the bakery door, stepping back out into the sea air that had noticeably warmed up while I was inside. The paper bag of remaining croissants was also warming my hand. As I started to make my way back home, I felt lighter somehow. The bakery visit had been nice. Normal. Maybe this new life wouldn't be so bad after all.

I decided to make a quick stop at the local market, remembering that I needed to stock up. The quaint little market was a stark contrast from the supermarkets I was used to, with its narrow aisles and creaky wooden floors. As I puzzled over unfamiliar local brands and squinted at handwritten price tags, a cheerful silver-haired cashier named Dorie came to my rescue. She patiently guided me through the store's offerings, even sneaking a few extra apples and a ripe peach into my bag "just for being new in town." By the time I left, arms laden with brown paper bags, I felt like I'd passed some sort of small-town initiation.

As I walked out of the market, a flash of color caught my eye. There, across the street, was Emma, her wild hair and colorful scarves unmistakable. She was staring directly at me, her expression unreadable behind her thick glasses.

Suddenly, her cryptic warning from earlier came flooding back. "Danger," she had said. "Dark clouds gathering on your horizon."

I shivered, despite the warmth of the morning sun. The comfortable feelings from the bakery and the local market evaporated, replaced by a creeping unease. What if Emma was right? What if there was something bad about to happen to me in the near future?

I quickened my pace, eager to get back to the relative safety of Martha's old house. As I hurried along, I could have sworn I felt Emma's eyes on my back. But when I chanced a glance over my shoulder, she had vanished as if she'd never been there at all.

The rest of the walk home was a blur, my mind racing with possibilities. Was I just being paranoid? Letting an old woman's ramblings get to me? Or was there really something to worry about?

As I fumbled with my keys at the front door, a neighbor across the street called out a friendly greeting. I managed a weak wave in return, but my heart wasn't in it. The warm glow of community I'd felt in the bakery had faded, replaced by a gnawing uncertainty.

I stepped inside, closing the door firmly behind me. The house suddenly felt like a sanctuary, a barrier between me and whatever dangers might be waiting for me outside.

"Calm down, Jim," I muttered to myself, setting the bags on the kitchen counter. "This isn't one of your mystery novels."

As I puttered around the kitchen, I tried to push Emma's warnings to the back of my mind. This was a charming town, filled with friendly people. What possible danger could there be?

Chapter 4

The rest of the day passed in another round of unpacking and arranging. By the time seven o'clock rolled around, I was surprisingly nervous about my evening plans with Peter. The thought of spending an evening talking to a stranger was more daunting than I cared to admit.

I changed into a fresh shirt and combed my thinning hair, chuckling at the absurdity of my nervousness. "It's just a beer with the neighbor, Jim," I muttered to my reflection. "Not a job interview."

The evening air was slightly cool as I made my way next door. Peter's house was similar to mine in structure, but far better maintained. The paint was fresh, the garden well-tended, and warm light spilled invitingly from the windows.

I had barely raised my hand to knock when the door swung open. Peter stood there, grinning broadly, a beer already in hand. "Jim! Right on time. Come on in, make yourself at home."

I stepped inside, immediately enveloped by the warmth and comfort of Peter's home. The house smelled faintly of wood smoke and something savory – a stark contrast to the musty scent of my own place.

"This is lovely," I said, taking in the tastefully decorated living room. Comfortable-looking leather armchairs were arranged around a crackling fireplace, and the walls were adorned with what looked like original paintings – seascapes and local landscapes, mostly.

Peter smiled, clearly pleased by my appreciation. "Thanks! I've put a fair bit of work into the place over the years. Here, let me grab you a beer."

As Peter disappeared into the kitchen, I found myself drawn to one of the paintings. It depicted a stormy sea, waves crashing against a rugged cliff face. Despite the tumultuous scene, there was something oddly soothing about it.

"That's one of my favorites," Peter said, returning with an opened bottle for me. "Reminds me of Oceanview Cove in a way."

I accepted the beer gratefully, taking a long swig. It was good – some kind of craft brew, much fancier than my usual fare. "You've got quite the eye for art," I commented.

Peter shrugged modestly. "That's just what I like. Come on, let's sit."

We settled into the armchairs, the fire crackling beside us. As we talked, I found myself relaxing. Peter was easy to chat with, full of funny stories about the town and its inhabitants. He had a way of telling a story that made you feel like you were in on some private joke, even if you'd never met the people involved.

A flash of movement caught my eye, and I looked down to see a large ginger cat winding its way between my legs.

"This is Ginger," Peter chuckled. "Don't let the name fool you – he's quite a terror when he wants to be."

I reached down to stroke the cat's head, and he immediately began to purr, loud enough to rival the crackling fire. "Seems friendly enough to me," I said.

Peter snorted. "Give it time, he's probably just sizing you up."

Despite Peter's warnings, Ginger seemed to like me. He hopped up onto my lap, kneading my legs for a moment before curling up into a contented ball. The warmth of the cat, combined with the cozy atmosphere and the beer, had me feeling more relaxed than I had in months.

"You know, Jim, I've been wondering," Peter said, leaning back in his chair. "Why did you decide to move to Oceanview Cove?"

I hesitated, unsure how much to share. But there was something about Peter's open, friendly face that invited confidence. "Well, it's a bit of a long story," I found myself saying. "My late wife Martha inherited that house from her parents years ago. She grew up here, you know, so we always talked about retiring here, but... well, life has a way of getting in the way of plans. After Martha was gone, it just felt right to fulfill that dream we'd had. The house, it's mine now, but it still feels like a part of her."

"I can understand that," Peter said softly, his eyes taking on a distant look. "You know, I remember Martha and her parents. We were neighbors back then. It must be hard, though. Living with all those memories."

I shrugged, feeling a familiar ache in my chest. "It is and it isn't. Sometimes it's a comfort, feeling close to her. Other times... well, let's just say it's an adjustment."

Peter raised his bottle. "To new beginnings, then. And to honoring the past."

I clinked my bottle against his, managing a small smile. "To new beginnings," I echoed.

Peter took a few sips of beer, his gaze distant as if lost in memory. After a long pause, he cleared his throat softly. "You know, Jim," he began, his voice tinged with a mix of nostalgia and hesitation, "I hope you don't mind me saying, but... Martha and I, we were more than neighbors. She was actually my first love, back in high school."

The comfortable warmth I'd been feeling evaporated in an instant, replaced by a cold, sick feeling in the pit of my stomach. "I'm sorry?"

Peter didn't seem to notice my discomfort. His eyes had taken on a faraway look, a small smile playing at the corners of his mouth. "We dated all through high school. God, she was something else. Smart as a whip, and pretty as a picture. Half the boys in town were in love with her, but somehow, I was the lucky one she chose."

I took a long swig of my beer, trying to quell the irrational surge of jealousy rising in my chest. This was ridiculous. Martha and I had been married for over forty years. What did it matter who she'd dated as a teenager?

But Peter was still talking, lost in his memories. "I remember our first date like it was yesterday. Took her to the local fair, tried to win her one of those giant stuffed animals. Ended up spending all my money and coming away with a tiny plastic keychain." He chuckled. "But Martha, bless her, acted like it was the best gift she'd ever gotten. Kept it on her schoolbag for the rest of the year."

I shifted uncomfortably in my seat, dislodging Ginger, who gave me an indignant look before stalking off towards the kitchen. "That's... that's a nice memory," I managed to say.

Peter nodded, taking another sip of his beer. "We were together right up until she left for college. Broke my heart when she went, but... well, I guess it all worked out in the end. She found you, after all."

There was something in his tone that set my teeth on edge. "Yes, well," I said curtly. "We had a good life together."

Peter's eyes snapped back to me, and I saw a flicker of realization cross his face. "Oh, Jim, I'm sorry. I didn't mean to... I mean, it must still be hard. It's only been a year, hasn't it?"

"A year," I said. "Look, Peter, I should probably be going. It's getting late, and I've still got a lot of unpacking to do."

I stood abruptly, nearly knocking over my half-full bottle of beer in the process. Peter looked startled by my sudden change in demeanor. "Are you sure? We've barely scratched the surface of my embarrassing high school stories."

"Another time, perhaps," I said, already moving towards the door. "Thank you for the beer."

Peter followed me, looking concerned. "Jim, I'm sorry if I upset you. I didn't mean to dredge up painful memories."

I paused at the door, feeling a twinge of guilt at my abrupt departure. Peter had been nothing but kind, after all. It wasn't his fault that his reminiscences had stirred up the feeling of jealousy in me. "It's fine," I said, not quite meeting his eyes. "Really. I'm just tired. It's been a long day."

Peter nodded, though he didn't look entirely convinced. "Of course. Well, we'll do this again some other time, yeah? Maybe we'll have something stronger than a beer."

I managed a weak smile. "That would be nice. Goodnight, Peter."

As I stepped out onto the porch, the cool evening air hit my flushed skin like a slap. I took a deep breath, trying to calm the swirling emotions in my chest.

"Everything okay, Jim?"

I jumped at the sound of Ryan's voice. He was lounging in a chair on his porch across the street, watching me with undisguised curiosity. How long had he been there?

"Fine," I said tersely. "Just heading home."

Ryan's eyebrows rose at my tone. "You sure? You look a bit... upset."

I forced myself to take another deep breath. I didn't want to alienate another neighbor. "Everything's fine," I repeated, trying to inject some warmth into my voice. "Just tired. You know how it is, moving and all."

Ryan nodded slowly, though his expression remained skeptical. "If you say so. Well, Jim, if you need anything, just tell me."

I muttered a tense "yes" and hurried across the lawn to my own house. As I fumbled with my keys, I could feel the weight of Ryan's gaze on my back. Combined with the lingering discomfort from Peter's stories, it made me feel exposed, vulnerable.

Finally, I got the door open and fled inside, shutting it firmly behind me. In the quiet darkness of the hallway, I leaned against the door, my heart pounding.

What was wrong with me? I'd overreacted, plain and simple. Peter had just been sharing memories, trying to make a connection. And I'd stormed out like a jealous teenager.

As I made my way upstairs to bed, I couldn't shake the uneasy feeling that had settled over me. Peter's stories had painted a picture of Martha I'd never known – young, carefree, and full of possibility. It made me aware of how much of her life I hadn't been a part of, how many experiences she'd had before we'd ever met.

And then there was the way Peter had talked about her, that hint of nostalgia in his voice. Was it possible that after all these years, he still carried a torch for his high school sweetheart?

I shook my head, trying to dispel the ridiculous thoughts. I was being paranoid, reading too much into innocent reminiscences. Martha had chosen me, after all. We'd built a life together, raised a daughter, shared countless moments of joy and sorrow. A teenage romance couldn't hold a candle to that.

Still, as I lay in bed that night, sleepless, I couldn't help but wonder what other surprises Oceanview Cove might have in store for me. I'd come here seeking peace and a connection to Martha's past. Instead, I seemed to be stirring up ghosts I wasn't sure I was prepared to face.

***

The next morning, I woke early, feeling groggy and out of sorts. The events of the previous evening weighed heavily on my mind as I went to the kitchen to make coffee.

As the kettle boiled, I peered out the window, half-expecting to see Ryan still sitting in his chair, watching. But the street was quiet, bathed in the soft light of dawn.

I took my coffee out to the porch, settling into the creaky rocking chair. The cool morning air helped clear my head, and I found myself feeling slightly embarrassed about my behavior the night before.

"You're going to have to apologize," I told myself. "Can't sour relations with the neighbors on your second day in town."

I decided to go over to Peter's later and smooth things over. Maybe I'd bring a peace offering – a bottle of wine, perhaps? Did Peter like wine? I realized how little I actually knew about my neighbor, despite our evening of conversation.

As I sat there, mulling over how to make amends, a movement across the street caught my eye. Ryan's front door opened, and he emerged, dressed in a slightly rumpled suit. He was carrying a leather briefcase and a mug of what I assumed was coffee.

Our eyes met, and for a moment, I tensed, expecting another probing question. But Ryan just gave me a cheerful wave before hurrying off down the street, probably heading to whatever passed for a newspaper office in a town this size.

I watched him go, feeling a mix of relief and guilt. Ryan had only been showing neighborly concern last night, and I'd brushed him off like an irritating fly.

"Add him to the apology list," I muttered, taking another sip of coffee.

The rest of the morning passed quietly. I busied myself with more arranging, trying to make the house feel more like home. And everywhere I turned, I was confronted with reminders of Martha – her books on the shelves, the faded photographs of her childhood still hanging on the walls.

It was nearing lunchtime when I finally worked up the courage to go over to Peter's. I'd bought a decent bottle of red wine in one of the colorful shops at the town center and hoped it would serve as a suitable peace offering.

I was halfway across my front lawn when I noticed something odd. Peter's curtains were still drawn, and his car was in the driveway, just where it had been the night before. Surely he wasn't still asleep?

A sense of unease began to creep over me as I approached Peter's front door. The house seemed too quiet, too still. I raised my hand to knock, but then hesitated. What if he was just a late sleeper? I didn't want to wake him.

But something felt wrong. Call it intuition, or maybe just the paranoia that had been following me since Emma's cryptic warning, but I couldn't shake the feeling that something was amiss.

I knocked, softly at first, then more firmly when there was no response. "Peter?" I called out. "It's Jim. I wanted to apologize for last night."

Silence.

I tried the doorknob, half-expecting it to be locked. To my surprise, it turned easily in my hand, and the door swung open.

"Peter?" I called again, stepping cautiously into the hallway. "Are you home?"

The house was silent, except for the soft ticking of a clock somewhere in the living room. I moved further inside, my unease growing with each step.

The living room looked much as it had the night before – cozy and inviting. But there was something off about it, something I couldn't quite put my finger on.

Then I saw it. A glass lay shattered on the floor near one of the armchairs, a dark stain spreading across the expensive-looking rug beneath it.

My heart began to race. "Peter!" I shouted. "Peter, are you all right?"

I rushed through the house, checking each room, my panic mounting with each empty space I encountered. Finally, I reached the kitchen.

There, sprawled on the floor beside the table, was Peter. A trail of dried foam crusted the corner of his mouth. I dropped to my knees beside his still form, my hands shaking as I reached out to touch him. Peter's skin was cool, his eyes staring blankly at the ceiling.

"Peter?" I whispered, my voice trembling. "Peter, can you hear me?"

There was no response. With a sense of growing dread, I pressed my fingers against his neck, searching for a pulse. I held my breath, praying to feel the faintest flutter beneath my fingertips.

Nothing.

I checked again, not wanting to believe it. But the stillness beneath my fingers confirmed my worst fear. Peter was dead.

Chapter 5

The next few hours passed in a blur. I called the police, my voice sounding strange and distant to my own ears as I reported finding Peter's body. After that, it was a whirlwind of activity – police cars with flashing lights, paramedics rushing in and out, curious neighbors gathering on the sidewalk.

I sat on my own porch, watching it all unfold feeling oddly disconnected from the moment. This couldn't be happening. Not here, not in this quaint little town where I'd come to find peace. And certainly not to Peter, who just last night had been so full of life, telling me the stories of his youth.

"Mr. Butterfield?"

I looked up to see a tall, broad-shouldered man in a sheriff's uniform standing before me. He had deep lines around his eyes that spoke more of frowns than laughter.

"I'm Sheriff Edward Miller," he said, his voice gruff but not unkind. "I need to ask you a few questions about what happened this morning."

I nodded numbly, gesturing to the chair beside me. But the sheriff shook his head.

"If you don't mind, sir, I'd prefer to do this inside. More private that way."

A chill ran down my spine at his words. More private or more intimidating? I pushed the thought aside and stood, leading the way into my house. The remaining half-unpacked boxes still littered the living room. What must the sheriff think of me, this newcomer living in chaos?

"Have a seat, Mr. Butterfield," Sheriff Miller said, gesturing to my armchair while remaining standing himself. The power dynamic was clear to me.

I sank into the chair, feeling oddly small. "What would you like to know, Sheriff?"

Miller pulled out a small notebook, flipping it open. "Let's start with the basics. When was the last time you saw Peter Johnson alive?"

"Last night," I said, my mouth dry. "He invited me over for a beer to welcome a new neighbor and all that."

The sheriff's eyebrows rose slightly. "And what time did you leave Mr. Johnson's house?"

I scratched my head, trying to remember. Everything from last night seemed hazy, overshadowed by the horror of this morning's discovery. "I'm not sure exactly. Maybe around nine? Nine-thirty?"

"Mhm," Miller grunted, scribbling in his notebook. "And how would you describe Mr. Johnson's state when you left? Was he upset? Agitated?"

I shook my head. "No, nothing like that. He seemed fine. A little nostalgic, maybe. We'd been talking about the past."

"The past?" The sheriff's piercing gaze fixed on me. "What about the past, exactly?"

I shifted uncomfortably in my seat. "Well, it turns out Peter knew my late wife when they were young. They... dated, apparently. In high school."

"I see." Miller's tone was neutral, but something in his expression made me nervous. "And how did that make you feel, Mr. Butterfield? Learning about your wife's past relationship with your new neighbor?"

The question caught me off guard. "I... well, I suppose I was a bit surprised. Maybe a little uncomfortable. But that's natural, isn't it?"

Miller didn't respond to that, just made another note in his notebook. "Mr. Butterfield, are you aware that you were likely the last person to see Peter Johnson alive?"

My stomach dropped. "I... no, I didn't realize that."

The sheriff's gaze became sharp as a knife. "We found two half-full beer bottles in Mr. Johnson's kitchen. Both had fingerprints on them."

"Well, yes," I said, trying to keep my voice steady. "As I said, we had a beer together. My fingerprints are probably on one of those bottles."

"Probably," Miller repeated, his tone making the word sound like an accusation. "We'll know for sure once the lab results come back."

I felt a flash of irritation cut through my anxiety. "Sheriff, surely you don't think I had anything to do with Peter's death? I barely knew the man. I just moved here!"

Miller's expression remained impassive. "Which makes you an unknown quantity, Mr. Butterfield. No history in town, no established relationships. Just a stranger who happens to be the last person to see the victim alive."

I gaped at him, unable to believe what I was hearing. "This is ridiculous! I'm just a retired librarian, for heaven's sake. I didn't kill anyone!"

"No one's accusing you of anything, sir," Miller said, his calm tone at odds with the suspicion in his eyes. "I'm just trying to establish the facts. Now, can you tell me your whereabouts between leaving Mr. Johnson's house last night and finding his body this morning?"

I took a deep breath, trying to calm myself. "I came straight home after leaving Peter's. Went to bed. Woke up this morning, had coffee on the porch. Then I went over to apologize to Peter. That's when I found him."

"Apologize?" Miller's eyebrows shot up. "What did you have to apologize for?"

I silently cursed myself for mentioning it. "It was nothing, really. I just... I left rather suddenly. The conversation about my wife had made me uncomfortable. I felt I'd been rude and wanted to smooth things over."

Miller made another note, his pen scratching loudly in the tense silence of the room. "I see. And did anyone see you come home last night? Anyone who can corroborate your story?"

I thought back to the previous evening, remembering Ryan's curious gaze as I'd hurried across my lawn. "Yes, actually. Ryan Perkins – he lives across the street. He was outside when I came home."

"Mhm," Miller grunted again. "We'll be sure to talk to Mr. Perkins."

He flipped his notebook closed, fixing me with one last penetrating stare. "I think that's all for now, Mr. Butterfield. But I'm sure we'll be speaking again soon. In the meantime, I'd advise you not to leave town."

The implication behind his words was clear. I was a suspect.

"This is absurd," I muttered, more to myself than to the sheriff. "I came here for a peaceful retirement, not to be accused of murder."

Miller paused at the door, turning back to me. "Retirement, you say? Bit of an odd choice, moving to a town where you don't know anyone. Most folks your age prefer to stay close to family."

There was something in his tone, a hint of suspicion that made my blood boil. "My wife grew up here," I said stiffly. "It was her dream to retire in her hometown. I'm fulfilling that dream for her."

"How nice," Miller said, his voice devoid of any real warmth. "Well, Mr. Butterfield, like I said – don't leave town. We'll be in touch."

With that, he was gone, leaving behind an uncomfortable silence that seemed to press in on me from all sides. I sank back into my chair, my head spinning.

How had this happened? Just yesterday, I'd been worried about making friends and settling into my new life. Now I was a murder suspect?

As the shock began to wear off, I felt a simmering anger rising in its place. The incompetence of it all! To suspect me, simply because I was new in town and had the misfortune to be Peter's last visitor? It was lazy police work, plain and simple.

I thought back to my interaction with Sheriff Miller, analyzing every question, every raised eyebrow. He'd been fishing, that was clear. Trying to trip me up, to catch me in a lie. But I had nothing to hide – except, perhaps, my own foolish jealousy over Peter's connection to Martha.

God, Martha. What would she think of all this? Her widower, suspected of murdering her high school sweetheart. It would have been laughable if it weren't so tragic.

I stood up, suddenly unable to sit still any longer. Pacing the room, I tried to make sense of the situation. Peter was dead – poisoned, most likely, given the state I'd found him in. But who would want to kill him? From what little I knew of Peter, he seemed well-liked in the community. Friendly, outgoing, with no obvious enemies.

Unless... A chilling thought struck me. What if Peter's death had nothing to do with Peter at all? What if it was connected to Emma's cryptic warning? "Danger," she had said. "Dark clouds gathering on your horizon."

I shook my head, trying to dispel the ridiculous notion. Emma was just a crazy old woman who thought she could read the future in the stars. Her "warning" was nothing more than a lucky guess, a vague prediction that could apply to any number of situations.

And yet... something didn't sit right. The charming seaside town suddenly felt like a stranger – one with dark secrets I was only beginning to notice.

For a moment, I considered calling Sarah. My fingers itched to dial her number, to share the bizarre turn of events and hear her reassuring voice. But as quickly as the thought came, I dismissed it. What would I say? That her retired father was now the prime suspect in a murder investigation? No, it was better not to worry her. I'd call her after this whole situation was resolved, when I could tell her about it as nothing more than an amusing anecdote about my new life in Oceanview Cove.

A sudden clatter from the kitchen snapped me out of my thoughts. I froze, my heart racing. Had Sheriff Miller come back? Or worse, was the real killer now in my house, looking to silence a potential witness?

I grabbed the nearest object – a heavy hardcover book – and crept towards the kitchen. As I approached, I heard a soft rustling, followed by what sounded like... chewing?

Peering around the doorframe, I blinked, certain I must be seeing things. There, perched on my kitchen counter, was Peter's ginger cat. And he was demolishing one of the croissants I'd bought from Maggie's bakery.

"Hey!" I exclaimed, more out of surprise than anger. "How did you get in here?"

The cat looked up, fixing me with a pair of sharp green eyes. And then, to my utter astonishment, it spoke.

"What are you looking at?" The words were clear as day, though they were accompanied by a sardonic meow.

I stumbled backwards, nearly dropping my impromptu weapon. "You... you can talk?"

The cat rolled its eyes – actually rolled its eyes – and went back to nibbling the croissant. "No, you're hallucinating. All the stress of being accused of murder has finally gotten to you."

I stared at the cat, my mind reeling. This couldn't be happening. Cats didn't talk. It was impossible. And yet...

"How..." I swallowed hard, trying to find my voice. "How can I understand you?"

The cat – Ginger, I remembered Peter calling him – shrugged in a surprisingly human-like gesture. "Beats me. Usually, only Peter could understand me. But I guess his ability somehow transferred to you since you were the last person to touch me before he kicked the bucket."

The casual way Ginger referred to Peter's death sent a chill down my spine. "You... you know what happened to Peter?"

Ginger's ears flattened against his head, and for the first time, I saw a flicker of genuine emotion in those feline eyes. "Yeah, I know. I was there."

I pulled out a kitchen chair and sank into it, my legs suddenly unable to support me. "Tell me everything," I said.

Ginger finished the last bite of croissant, licking crumbs from his whiskers. "Not much to tell, really. I was asleep for most of it. Woke up to the sound of Peter hitting the floor. By the time I got to the kitchen, he was already gone."

"But surely you must have seen something," I pressed. "Heard something?"

The cat's tail twitched irritably. "I told you, I was asleep. Cats sleep a lot, in case you hadn't noticed." He paused, seeming to consider. "Although... I did see something when I looked out the window. A shadow, moving away from the house. Couldn't tell who it was, though. It quickly disappeared into the night."

My mind was racing. A shadow leaving the house – that had to be the killer. "What time was this?" I asked.

Ginger gave me a look that clearly questioned my intelligence. "I'm a cat. We don't wear watches."

I sighed, pinching the bridge of my nose. This was surreal. I was interrogating a cat about a murder. If I wasn't careful, I'd end up as the town lunatic instead of just the town murder suspect.

"Okay, let's back up," I said. "You said only Peter could understand you before. Why is that?"

Ginger stretched languorously before settling into a more comfortable position on the counter. "Look, I've always been able to understand you humans yammering on. But Peter was special. He was the only one who could understand *me*. He found me as a kitten, half-dead in a gutter. Nursed me back to health. After that, we just... clicked. He called it a 'psychic bond' or some such nonsense. I just figured he was less dense than most humans."

I nodded slowly, trying to process this information. "And now that... 'psychic bond' has somehow transferred to me? Because I was the last to touch you before Peter died?"

Ginger's tail twitched irritably. "Your guess is as good as mine, Watson. All I know is, one minute I'm discovering my human's cold body on the kitchen floor, the next I'm having a chat with a retired librarian. So yeah, seems like you've inherited Peter's 'gift' of understanding me. Lucky you."

I couldn't tell if he was being sarcastic or not. Probably. He seemed to have a talent for it. But as far-fetched as this explanation was, it was the only one we had. For now, at least, we'd have to work with it.

"So," I said, leaning forward. "You want to help me figure out who killed Peter?"

Ginger's eyes narrowed. "What's in it for me?"

I blinked, taken aback. Apparently, finding a killer of his friend wasn't motivation enough. "I... what do you want?"

The cat seemed to consider this for a moment. "A warm place to sleep, regular meals, and..." his eyes flickered to the empty plate that had held the croissant, "a steady supply of those delicious pastries from the bakery."

Despite the gravity of the situation, I felt a smile tugging at the corners of my mouth. "Deal."

Ginger hopped down from the counter, walking over to where I sat. He looked up at me, his expression suddenly serious. "Look, old man. I liked Peter. He was good to me. If you're going to find out who did this to him, I want in. But let's get one thing straight – I'm not your pet. We're partners in this, got it?"

I nodded, feeling a strange mix of amusement and determination. "Got it. Partners."

And just like that, I found myself forming an unlikely alliance with a talking cat to solve a murder and clear my name. If someone had told me yesterday that this would be my situation, I'd have thought they were crazy. Now, I wasn't so sure I wasn't the crazy one.

"So," I said, trying to gather my thoughts. "Where do we start?"

Ginger's whiskers twitched in what I was beginning to recognize as his version of a smirk. "Well, partner, I'd say we start by making a list of suspects. And in a town like this, with more secrets than a teenage girl's diary, that might take a while."

I couldn't help but chuckle at the cat's sardonic tone. "You sound like you know a lot about the people in this town."

"You'd be surprised what people say and do when they think only a cat is watching," Ginger replied, his tail swishing mischievously. "I've got dirt on half the residents of Oceanview Cove."

"Alright then," I said, reaching for a pen and paper. "Let's hear it. Who do you think might have wanted Peter dead?"

For the next half an hour, Ginger and I compiled a list of potential suspects, complete with possible motives. The cat's insider knowledge was surprising and, frankly, a little disturbing. Who knew that Mrs. Henderson from three doors down was having an affair with the milkman? Or that the town's respected doctor had a gambling problem?

"None of this explains why someone would want to kill Peter, though," I said, frowning at our list.

Ginger stretched out on the kitchen table, his tail curling around my coffee mug. "Maybe not directly, but it gives us a starting point. People with secrets are dangerous, old man. They'll do anything to keep those secrets buried."

I nodded. "You're right. And if we're going to get to the bottom of this, we need to start digging."

"Now you're talking," Ginger said, a glint in his eyes. "But first, I think we need to pay a visit to the Salty Breeze, our local bar."

I raised an eyebrow. "Why?"

Ginger's whiskers twitched. "Because, my dear Watson, Peter was a regular there. And in my experience, bartenders know more about people's secrets than anyone else in town. More than even me, if you can believe it. Not that I cared much about Peter's secrets. He kept his business to himself, and I was too busy napping to play detective."

As bizarre as this situation was, I had to admit Ginger had a point. The bar could be a goldmine of information about Peter and his relationships in town.

"Alright," I said, standing up. "Let's go to the Salty Breeze."

As I grabbed my coat and headed for the door, Ginger cleared his throat – or whatever the feline equivalent was. "Uh, forgetting something?"

I turned back, confused. "What?"

He fixed me with a stern look. "You can't just walk into a bar with a cat, old man. We need a plan."

I couldn't help but chuckle. "Right. Any suggestions?"

Ginger's tail swished thoughtfully. "I'll follow you and sneak in. You just focus on getting the bartender to talk. And remember, I'll be listening to everything, so don't mess it up."

As we left the house, I marveled at the turn my life had taken. Twenty-four hours ago, I was worried about making friends in my new town. Now, I was embarking on a murder investigation with a talking cat as my sidekick.

"You know," I said as we walked, "when I decided to move here for a quiet retirement, this isn't exactly what I had in mind."

Ginger looked up at me, amusement glinting in his green eyes. "Welcome to Oceanview Cove, old man. Where the sea is blue, the secrets are dark, and nothing is ever quite what it seems."

As we made our way down the street, drawing curious glances from neighbors who no doubt wondered why the town's newest resident and murder suspect was out for a stroll with a cat, I couldn't shake the feeling that this was only the beginning. But one thing was clear: I couldn't just sit back and wait for Sheriff Miller to decide my fate. If I wanted to clear my name, I was going to have to get to the bottom of what had happened to Peter.

The thought was both terrifying and oddly exciting. I'd spent my entire career surrounded by mystery novels, losing myself in stories of amateur sleuths and brilliant detectives. Now, it seemed, I was about to step into my very own whodunit.

Chapter 6

I approached the Salty Breeze with Ginger walking silently beside me. The weathered wooden sign creaked in the sea breeze, its faded letters barely legible. As we neared the entrance, a burly man with arms like tree trunks stepped into our path.

"Evening," he grunted, eyeing Ginger suspiciously. "No pets allowed inside."

I opened my mouth to respond, but Ginger beat me to it with an indignant hiss. "Who are you calling a pet, you overgrown gorilla?" he said. The guard, of course, only heard an angry meow.

"He's not exactly a pet," I started to say, but the guard shook his head firmly.

"Rules are rules, sir. The cat stays outside."

I glanced down at Ginger, who was glaring daggers at the guard. "Do like we discussed," I murmured quietly.

Ginger's tail twitched in annoyance, but he gave a barely perceptible nod before slinking off into the shadows.

I turned back to the guard with an apologetic smile. "Sorry about that. He's not used to being left behind. I'll just be a few minutes, have a couple of pints, you know?"

The guard grunted again but stepped aside to let me pass. As I entered the bar, I made a show of patting my pockets and looking confused. "Oh, drat," I muttered loudly. "I think I dropped my wallet outside."

While the guard's attention was diverted, I caught a glimpse of an orange blur darting through the door. Ginger had made it inside. I breathed a sigh of relief and turned to take in my surroundings.

The Salty Breeze lived up to its name. The air was thick with the smell of stale beer and salt, mingled with the faint aroma of fried food. Warm, dim lighting cast long shadows across the room, illuminating the faded nautical maps and old fishing gear that adorned the walls. The low murmur of conversation was punctuated by the occasional clink of glasses and bursts of laughter.

As I made my way to the bar, I felt the weight of suspicious glances from the other patrons. News traveled fast in small towns, and I was willing to bet that everyone here knew about Peter's death – and my possible involvement.

I settled onto a worn wooden stool at the bar, trying to ignore the prickle of eyes on my back. A movement caught my attention, and I spotted Ginger weaving his way between tables, somehow managing to avoid detection.

"What'll it be, stranger?"

I turned to find myself face to face with a silver-haired older man behind the bar. His face was a roadmap of wrinkles, each one seeming to tell a story of its own. Despite his age, his eyes were sharp and alert, taking in every detail.

"Just a beer, please," I said. Then, remembering what Ginger had told me earlier, I added, "You must be Shawn. I hear you're quite famous in town."

The bartender's bushy eyebrows rose slightly. "That I am. And you must be Jim Butterfield. Heard you moved into Martha Parker's old place."

I nodded, surprised. "Word gets around fast, doesn't it?"

Shawn chuckled, sliding a mug of beer in front of me. "Small town, big ears. Especially when there's a story as interesting as yours."

I took a long swig of beer, bracing myself for the accusation I was sure was coming. But Shawn surprised me.

"For what it's worth," he said, leaning in conspiratorially, "I don't believe for a second you had anything to do with Peter's death."

I blinked, taken aback by his frankness. "You don't?"

Shawn shook his head. "Nah. I knew Martha's parents, you see. They were good people. And Martha, she wouldn't have married a man who wasn't cut from the same cloth."

I felt a sudden swell of emotion at Shawn's words. I took another drink, hoping to mask the slight tremor in my voice. "Thank you," I managed. "That... means a lot."

Shawn waved off my thanks. "Just calling it like I see it. Now," his eyes twinkled mischievously, "what did you do before retiring to our quaint little seaside town?"

"I was a librarian," I admitted.

Shawn's face lit up. "A librarian! Well, why didn't you say so? I've got just the thing for you." He turned to the bottles lining the back wall, grabbing several with practiced ease. "You're in luck. I've been working on a new cocktail, and I think you're just the man to give it a try."

I watched, fascinated, as Shawn's hands flew over the bottles, pouring and mixing with the skill of a master alchemist. Finally, he placed a glass in front of me with a flourish. The drink inside was a deep amber color, with what looked like a twisted lemon peel floating on top.

"I call it 'The Librarian,'" Shawn announced proudly.

I raised an eyebrow. "The Librarian? Did you just come up with that name?"

Shawn winked. "Maybe I did, maybe I didn't. A good bartender never reveals all his secrets. Go on, give it a try."

I lifted the glass cautiously and took a sip. The flavor was complex – a hint of whiskey, something citrusy, and an underlying sweetness that I couldn't quite place. It was surprisingly good.

"Well?" Shawn asked eagerly.

"It's delicious," I said honestly. "What's in it?"

Shawn winked again. "Ah, that's also a secret. But I'm glad you like it. Consider it on the house – a proper welcome to Oceanview Cove."

As I sipped my drink, I noticed Ginger had managed to position himself under a nearby table, his green eyes fixed on me intently. Right. We were here for a reason.

"Shawn," I said, trying to keep my tone casual, "you must have known Peter pretty well. He was a regular here, wasn't he?"

The bartender's expression sobered. "Aye, that he was. Came in most evenings for a pint or two. Terrible business, what happened to him."

I nodded sympathetically. "When was the last time you saw him?"

Shawn's brow furrowed in thought. "Would've been... four nights ago, I reckon. Which was odd, now that I think about it. Peter never missed that many nights in a row."

"Did he seem... different that night?" I pressed. "Upset about anything?"

Shawn gave me a sharp look. "You asking just out of curiosity, or is this about finding out what happened to him?"

I felt my face heat up. "Both, I suppose," I admitted. "I barely knew Peter, but he seemed like a good man. And..." I trailed off, unsure how to explain my situation without sounding crazy.

Shawn nodded slowly. "Fair enough. To answer your question, yes, Peter did seem a bit off that night. Distracted, I'd say. Kept looking over his shoulder, as if he expected someone to jump out at him."

My pulse quickened. This could be important. "Did he say anything about why he was worried?"

Shawn shook his head. "Not in so many words. But he did mention having an argument with Robert earlier that day."

"Robert?" I asked.

"Robert Reeves," Shawn clarified. "Local fisherman. Grumpy sort, but usually keeps to himself. But the way Peter talked, sounds like they had quite the dust-up."

I leaned forward, intrigued. "What were they arguing about?"

Shawn shrugged. "Peter didn't say, exactly. But whatever it was, it had him rattled."

I nodded, making a mental note. Robert Reeves was definitely someone I needed to talk to.

"This Robert," I said carefully, "what's he like? Do you think he could have..." I let the question hang in the air.

Shawn's eyes narrowed. "Robert? He's got a temper on him, that's for sure. But murder? I don't know, Jim. That's a big leap."

I nodded, trying not to show my excitement at this potential lead.

As if sensing my thoughts, Shawn leaned in closer. "Look, Jim. I don't know what really happened to Peter. But I do know this town. Secrets have a way of bubbling to the surface here, sooner or later. Just keep your eyes and ears open, and you might be surprised what you learn."

I finished my drink, mulling over Shawn's words. As I stood to leave, I felt something brush against my leg. Ginger had materialized beside me, somehow managing to look both smug and impatient.

"Thanks for the drink, Shawn," I said. "And for the talk. I appreciate it."

Shawn waved me off with a smile. "Anytime, Jim. And hey," he called as I turned to go, "don't let the gossips get you down. This town's full of good people. You'll see."

As Ginger and I slipped out of the bar, narrowly avoiding the guard's notice, I couldn't help but feel a mixture of hope and apprehension. We had a lead – Robert Reeves – but I had a feeling we were only scratching the surface of Oceanview Cove's secrets.

As we made our way down the street, Peter's house came into view. Yellow police tape still encircled the property, a bored-looking police officer stood sentinel near the front door. The house seemed to loom in the fading light, its windows dark and accusing.

"They're not taking any chances, are they?" I murmured to Ginger.

He flicked his tail dismissively. "Locking the barn door after the horse has bolted, if you ask me. At this rate, the only evidence they'll find is last week's forgotten grocery list."

As we reached my front porch, Ginger fixed me with a penetrating stare. "Well," he said, his tail twitching impatiently, "are you going to tell me what you learned, or do I have to guess?"

I sighed, pulling out my keys. "It's going to be a long night," I muttered. Then, feeling the weight of the day settling on my shoulders, I added, "But nap first."

Chapter 7

I woke with a start, sunlight streaming through the curtains I'd forgotten to close. My brief nap had turned into a full night's sleep.

"About time you woke up," Ginger's voice came from somewhere near my feet. I looked down to see him perched on the edge of the bed, tail swishing impatiently. "I was starting to wonder if I'd need to learn how to dial 911 with my paws."

I groaned, pushing myself up. My back protested the movement, reminding me that I wasn't as young as I used to be. "What time is it?"

"Time for breakfast," Ginger replied, jumping off the bed. "I don't know if you've noticed, but I don't have opposable thumbs. Feeding myself is a bit of a challenge."

I shuffled to the kitchen, Ginger weaving between my legs in a way that threatened to send me sprawling. After a quick rummage through the cupboards, I found a can of tuna that seemed to meet with Ginger's approval. While Ginger tucked into his breakfast, I set about making myself a much-needed cup of coffee. The rich aroma filled the kitchen as the coffee brewed, helping to clear the fog from my mind.

As I watched Ginger devour his breakfast, coffee mug in hand, I remembered our rushed conversation before yesterday's 'quick nap' turned into a full night's sleep. I'd told Ginger about my chat with Shawn at the bar, but I'd never gotten around to asking about his own reconnaissance because I'd simply passed out.

I took a sip of coffee, then asked, "By the way, did you manage to overhear anything useful back at the bar last night?"

Ginger paused, licking a bit of tuna off his whiskers. "Useful? Not particularly. Mostly just gossip and people talking about you. You wouldn't believe some of the ridiculous theories they've come up with."

I raised an eyebrow. "Like what?"

"Oh, you know," Ginger said, his tail twitching in amusement. "The usual small-town nonsense. Some think you're a secret government agent. Others are convinced you're Peter's long-lost brother, here to claim your inheritance. My personal favorite is that you're actually a famous author researching your next murder mystery."

I couldn't help but chuckle. "Well, at least they're being creative."

As amusing as the town's wild theories about me were, they weren't going to help us solve Peter's murder. I took a sip of my coffee, letting the bitter warmth clear the last cobwebs of sleep from my mind.

"So," I said, bringing the conversation back on track, "what's the plan for today?"

Ginger looked up, a bit of tuna stuck to his whiskers. "We need to talk to Robert Reeves. He's usually down at the docks this time of morning."

I nodded. "Right. The grumpy fisherman Shawn mentioned. You think he might know something about Peter's death?"

"Maybe," Ginger said, licking his paw. "Or maybe he is the killer. Either way, he's our best lead right now."

As we made our way to the docks, the town was just beginning to wake up. The air was crisp with the promise of another warm day, carrying the mingled scents of salt water and fresh bread from Maggie's bakery. Shopkeepers swept their storefronts, exchanging cheerful greetings with early-rising neighbors. A group of schoolchildren on their way to class laughed and chattered, their voices echoing off the colorful facades of the buildings lining the narrow streets.

The closer we got to the waterfront, the more the quaint charm of the town center gave way to the rugged practicality of a working harbor. The smell of fish and diesel fuel grew stronger, and the cheerful voices were replaced by the rumble of boat engines.

The Oceanview Cove docks came into view, a jumble of weathered wood and salt-stained ropes. Fishing boats bobbed gently in the harbor, their colorful hulls a stark contrast to the deep blue of the water. The air was thick with the smell of brine and fish, punctuated by the raucous cries of seagulls flying overhead.

"There," Ginger said, nodding towards a stocky man wrestling with a pile of nets on the deck of an old fishing boat. "That's Robert."

I hesitated for a moment, eyeing the gentle rocking of the vessel. It had been years since I'd set foot on a boat, and my balance wasn't what it used to be. But there was no help for it. Taking a deep breath, I stepped onto the gangplank and carefully made my way aboard, Ginger following with feline grace.

I approached cautiously, aware of the knife hanging from Robert's belt. He looked up as I neared, his face twisted into a scowl.

"What do you want?" he growled, not pausing in his work.

I cleared my throat. "Mr. Reeves? I'm Jim Butterfield. I was hoping I could ask you a few questions about Peter Johnson."

Robert's hands stilled for a moment, his eyes narrowing. "You're the new guy. The one they think killed Peter."

It wasn't a question, but I nodded anyway. "That's right. But I didn't kill him, which is why I'm trying to figure out who did."

Robert snorted, turning back to his nets. "And what makes you think I know anything about it?"

"Oh, I don't know," Ginger muttered sarcastically. "Maybe the fact that you look guiltier than a kid with his hand in the cookie jar?"

I took a deep breath, steeling myself. "I heard you and Peter had an argument a few days before he died. I was wondering if you could tell me what it was about."

The change in Robert's demeanor was immediate. His shoulders tensed, and when he looked at me again, his eyes were blazing. "It was nothing," he spat. "Just a disagreement between neighbors. Happens all the time."

"A disagreement that left Peter rattled?" I pressed, remembering Shawn's words.

"Right," Ginger snorted. "Because everyone gets 'rattled' over nothing."

Robert took a step towards me, his fists clenched at his sides. "Listen here, old man. I don't know what you think you're doing, playing detective, but you'd best mind your own business. I had nothing to do with Peter's death, you hear me? Nothing."

"I'm not accusing you of anything, Mr. Reeves. I'm just trying to understand what happened."

"Well, understand this," Robert snarled. "I'm done talking. Now get off my boat before I throw you off."

"Charming fellow," Ginger remarked dryly. "I can see why he's so popular in town."

I backed away, nearly tripping over a coil of rope. As I steadied myself, I noticed a table near the boat's cabin.

Among the usual fishing paraphernalia lay a large knife, its blade dark with what looked like blood.

Before I could comment, Ginger darted past me, leaping onto the table. He sniffed at the knife, his whiskers twitching.

"Hey!" Robert shouted, lunging for Ginger. "Get that mangy cat off my boat!"

Ginger dodged Robert's grasp, jumping back to the dock. He looked up at me, his green eyes wide. "Jim, that knife-"

"It's just a filleting knife," I said quickly, hoping Robert hadn't noticed me apparently talking to a cat. "Probably used to gut fish this morning."

Robert glared at us both. "That's right. Not that it's any of your business. Now get out of here, both of you."

As we hurried away from the docks, I could feel Robert's eyes burning into my back. Once we were out of earshot, I turned to Ginger. "What were you thinking? You could have gotten us both thrown into the harbor!"

Ginger sat down, calmly grooming his paw. "I was thinking that the knife might be evidence. But you're right, it's just fish blood. I could smell it."

I sighed, running a hand through my thinning hair. "Even if it wasn't, Peter was poisoned, remember? He wasn't stabbed."

"True," Ginger conceded. "But Robert is definitely hiding something. Did you see how he reacted when you mentioned the argument?"

I nodded, glancing back towards the docks. Robert had returned to his work, but his movements seemed more agitated than before. "He's certainly not winning any awards for openness. But that doesn't make him a killer."

"No," Ginger agreed. "But it does make him suspicious. What do you think they were arguing about?"

I shrugged. "Could be anything. But whatever it was, it seems to have Robert pretty worked up."

Ginger trotted alongside me, his tail held high. "There's got to be more to it."

As we walked, I mulled over our encounter with Robert. His reaction had been extreme, no doubt about it. But was it the reaction of a guilty man, or just someone with a short temper who didn't like being questioned?

"We need more information," I said finally. "Robert's not going to tell us anything willingly. We need to find out more about him, about his relationship with Peter."

Ginger nodded. "Agreed. But how? It's not like we can go around asking people without raising suspicion. In case you've forgotten, you're still the prime suspect in a murder investigation."

I grimaced. How could I forget? The weight of suspicion had been hanging over me since I'd found Peter's body. But Ginger had a point. We needed to be careful about how we gathered information.

As we made our way back from the docks, the afternoon sun bathed Oceanview Cove in a warm, golden glow. The narrow, cobblestone streets echoed with the rhythmic clip-clop of my shoes and Ginger's soft paws. Quaint storefronts and colorful houses lined our path, their cheerful facades in glaring contrast with the tension we'd just experienced with Robert Reeves.

Suddenly, I spotted a familiar figure up ahead. Emma, the eccentric astrologer I'd met on my first day in town, was emerging from a shop, her arms laden with paper bags.

"Oh no," I muttered under my breath.

Ginger looked up at me, his tail twitching curiously. "What's wrong? You look like you've seen a ghost."

I quickly filled Ginger in on my previous encounter with Emma, telling about her cryptic warnings and the strange "protective" stone she'd given me.

Ginger's whiskers twitched in what I was beginning to recognize as his version of a smirk. "Ah, our crazy town astrologer. Let me guess – she told you Mercury was in retrograde and that's why you can't find matching socks?"

I chuckled despite myself. "Not quite. She warned me about 'danger' and 'dark clouds gathering on my horizon.' I thought she was just being dramatic, but now..."

"Now you're wondering if she might have been onto something," Ginger finished for me. He shook his head. "Don't tell me you're starting to believe in that mumbo-jumbo."

Before I could respond, Emma spotted us. Her face lit up with recognition, and she began making her way towards us, her colorful scarves trailing behind her like exotic bird feathers.

"Jim Butterfield!" she called out, her voice carrying down the street. "The stars told me our paths would cross again soon!"

Ginger snorted. "Did they now? How convenient."

I shot Ginger a warning look as Emma approached. Up close, she looked even more eccentric than I remembered. Today, her silver hair was woven into intricate braids, each one tipped with a different colored bead that clinked softly as she moved.

"Hello, Emma," I greeted her, trying to keep my voice neutral. "How are you?"

Emma's eyes, magnified by her thick glasses, darted between me and Ginger. "Oh, I'm quite well, thank you. But more importantly, how are you, Jim? Have you been heeding my warning?"

I shifted uncomfortably. "About that, Emma... I was wondering if you could tell me more about what you meant. How did you know something bad was going to happen?"

Emma's expression turned serious. She glanced around furtively, as if checking for eavesdroppers, before leaning in close. "The stars, Jim. They speak to those who know how to listen. And lately, they've been practically shouting."

Ginger made a sound that was suspiciously like a stifled laugh. Emma's gaze snapped to him, her eyes narrowing slightly.

"Your cat," she said slowly. "He's not what he seems, is he?"

I felt a jolt of panic. Could Emma somehow sense our so-called 'psychic bond'? "He's just a regular cat," I said quickly. "Nothing special about him."

Ginger looked up at me, his expression clearly saying, "Speak for yourself, old man."

Emma shook her head. "No, no. There's something... different about him. The stars whisper of hidden truths and unexpected allies." She fixed her gaze on me again. "Which brings me to my warning, Jim. Be careful of people pretending to be something they're not."

I blinked, taken aback by the sudden shift. "What do you mean?"

"Exactly what I said," Emma replied cryptically. "Not everyone in Oceanview Cove is what they appear to be. Some wear masks so convincing, they've even fooled themselves."

Ginger's tail swished impatiently. I could almost hear his sarcastic comment about Emma's vague warnings.

"Emma," I said, trying to keep my frustration in check, "I appreciate your concern, but could you be more specific? Are you talking about someone in particular?"

Emma's gaze became distant. "I see... a man of the sea, but his waters run deep and dark." She blinked, her eyes refocusing on me. "The stars don't always speak plainly, Jim. It's up to us to interpret their messages."

I suppressed a sigh. This was getting us nowhere. "Right. Well, thank you for the... insight, Emma. I'll be sure to keep my eyes open."

Emma nodded sagely. "See that you do, Jim. Oh, and one more thing." She reached into one of her bags and pulled out a small, violet stone. "Keep this with you. Amethyst – for protection and clarity of mind. You're going to need both in the coming days."

Before I could protest, she pressed the stone into my hand. Its surface was cool and smooth against my palm.

"Thanks," I mumbled, not knowing what else to say.

Emma beamed at me, then turned her attention to Ginger. "And you, little one. Keep a close eye on your friend here. He's going to need all the help he can get."

With that, she gathered up her bags and continued down the street, her scarves fluttering behind her like colorful smoke.

Once Emma had disappeared around the corner, Ginger let out a long, low meow that sounded suspiciously like a groan. "Well, that was... something. Do all your conversations with her end with you acquiring new paperweights?"

I looked down at the amethyst in my hand, then slipped it into my pocket alongside the lodestone Emma had given me before. "She means well, I think. She's just a bit..."

"Nutty as a fruitcake?" Ginger supplied helpfully.

I couldn't help but chuckle. "I was going to say 'eccentric,' but your description works too."

We continued our walk back home, the afternoon sun beaming down from a cloudless sky. Despite my attempt at humor, Emma's words niggled at the back of my mind.

"You don't think..." I began, then shook my head. "No, never mind. It's ridiculous."

Ginger looked up at me, his green eyes gleaming in the fading light. "What's ridiculous? The fact that you're starting to take the ramblings of a woman who probably reads tea leaves for a living seriously?"

I sighed. "When you put it like that, it does sound absurd. But you have to admit, some of what she said... it fits. A man of the sea with dark waters? That could be Robert Reeves."

"Or the king of Atlantis," Ginger retorted. "These kinds of vague predictions can fit anyone if you try hard enough. It's called cold reading, Jim. Don't fall for it."

I nodded, trying to shake off the lingering unease. "You're right, of course. We need to focus on facts, not fortune-telling."

But as we reached my front porch, I couldn't help but touch the amethyst in my pocket. Crazy or not, Emma had been right about one thing – danger had found its way to Oceanview Cove. And somehow, I'd landed right in the middle of it.

Chapter 8

I slumped into my armchair, the events of the day weighing heavily on my mind. The warm afternoon sun shone through the windows, casting long shadows across the living room. Dust motes danced in the golden beams, a silent reminder of all the household chores I'd been neglecting. The faded wallpaper, a relic from Martha's parents' time, seemed to absorb the light, giving the room a soft, nostalgic glow.

Ginger leapt onto the coffee table, his orange fur catching the sunlight and almost glowing. His green eyes fixed on me with an intensity that still caught me off guard. "Well, that was an interesting day," he said, his tail swishing back and forth.

I snorted, the sound loud in the quiet room. "That's one way to put it. I feel like I've stumbled into one of those mystery novels I used to read in the library."

The thought triggered a memory of an old Agatha Christie book – "The Murder of Roger Ackroyd." I'd always admired how Christie wove complex webs of deceit and misdirection. Now, finding myself in the middle of a real-life murder mystery, I couldn't help but wonder if I was missing some vital clue, just like her narrator had. The weight of the responsibility settled on my shoulders, making me sink deeper into the worn cushions of the armchair.

Shaking off the literary comparison, I focused back on Ginger. His whiskers twitched as if he could sense my thoughts. "You know, it occurs to me that you probably know more about Peter than anyone else in this town. What can you tell me about him?"

Ginger's whiskers twitched again, this time in what I was beginning to recognize as amusement. "Ah, Peter. He was... complicated. Not at all what he seemed on the surface."

"How so?" I leaned forward, intrigued, the old springs of the armchair creaking under my shifting weight.

"Well, for starters, he wasn't nearly as sociable as he appeared. Sure, he'd chat with the neighbors and go to the bar, but at home? He was a different man entirely."

I frowned, the wrinkles on my forehead deepening. "Different how?"

Ginger settled into a more comfortable position, his paws tucked neatly under him. "He was restless. Paced a lot, especially at night. The floorboards would creak under his constant movement. He had a habit of talking to himself when he thought no one was listening, muttering under his breath like he was working out some complex problem. And he was always on that computer of his, typing away like his life depended on it. The click-clack of the keys was like a constant backdrop to the house."

"Did you ever see what he was working on?"

Ginger shook his head. "Not clearly. We had a special connection, sure, but that didn't mean he told me everything. He was careful about what he let slip, even around me. Always closing the browser when I jumped up on the desk and playing those stupid fish tank videos for me. Don't know why I always fell for those, though."

I nodded, processing this information. I had no clue what these fish tank videos were, but Peter's secrecy painted a picture markedly different from the friendly neighbor I'd met. "What about visitors? Did he have many people come by?"

Ginger's green eyes narrowed in thought. "Not many regulars, no. But there were these meetings..."

"Meetings?" I prompted when he trailed off, leaning forward.

"Yes. Every so often, people I didn't recognize would come to the house. Definitely not locals. Their clothes were too crisp, too new. They smelled of the city, not of sea salt and fish. Peter would take them into his study and close the door. I couldn't hear much, but the conversations always seemed... intense. Voices would rise and fall, though I could never make out the words."

With Ginger's revelations, my mind raced with possibilities. What kind of business had Peter been involved in? And could it have led to his death? The situation reminded me of another mystery novel I'd read years ago – "The Big Sleep" by Raymond Chandler. In that story, the detective had also stumbled upon a web of secrets and lies that went far deeper than he'd initially suspected. Now, I couldn't help but wonder if I was in for a similar journey.

"Ginger," I said slowly, an idea forming, "these meetings were in Peter's study, right?"

Ginger nodded, his eyes gleaming with interest. "Yes, why?"

I stood up, pacing the room as I thought aloud. "If Peter was involved in something... questionable, there might be evidence in that study. Documents, maybe, or something that could point us towards what really happened to him."

Ginger's tail swished excitedly, stirring up more dust motes. "Now you're thinking like a proper detective, old man. One problem, though – the police have Peter's house locked up tight. How do you propose we get in?"

I stopped pacing, a smile tugging at the corners of my mouth. "We don't. But you could."

Ginger's ears perked up, swiveling towards me like little satellite dishes. "Oh? Do tell."

"You're a cat," I explained, warming to my plan. "Small, agile, able to slip through tight spaces. If you could find a way into the house, you could search Peter's study without anyone noticing."

I paused, another idea striking me. "And you know what? I could help create a distraction. There's a police officer stationed near the front door. I could engage him in conversation, maybe ask some questions about the investigation. While he's occupied with me, you could slip inside unnoticed."

Ginger's whiskers twitched in what I was learning to recognize as his version of a grin. "Sneaking into places I'm not supposed to be? That's practically in my job description as a cat. And with you running interference? This would be a walk in the park."

As I outlined my plan, I couldn't help but reflect on the absurdity of the situation. Here I was, a retired librarian, plotting a break-in with a talking cat. If someone had told me a week ago that this would be my life, I'd have laughed them out of the room.

But then again, isn't that how all great mysteries start? With an ordinary person thrust into extraordinary circumstances? I thought of Miss Marple, Christie's unassuming elderly sleuth. She'd solved countless crimes armed with nothing but her wits and her understanding of human nature. Perhaps, with Ginger's help, I could do the same.

"So you'll do it?" I asked.

Ginger stood, stretching languidly, his claws extending and retracting. "Of course. It's not like I have a busy social calendar to clear. When do we start?"

I glanced out the window. The setting sun bathed the sky in vibrant oranges and pinks. The sea in the distance sparkled like scattered gemstones. "It'll be dark soon. That should give you plenty of cover. Think you can manage it tonight?"

Ginger's tail swished mischievously. "Please. I once stole an entire salmon from Mrs. Henderson's kitchen without leaving a single paw print. This will be a breeze."

After giving Ginger an evening snack to fuel his upcoming midnight reconnaissance, I found myself both excited and apprehensive. What secrets would we uncover in Peter's study? Would they lead us to the killer, or just deeper into the mystery?

I sank back into my chair, my mind whirling with possibilities. The last rays of sunlight faded from the room, leaving only shadows that seemed to mirror the murky depths of the case we were diving into. As darkness fell, I couldn't shake the feeling that we were about to cross a line. But then again, I reminded myself, I was already the prime suspect in a murder investigation. How much worse could things get?

Little did I know, I was about to find out.

Chapter 9

The moon hung low in the sky, its pale light filtering through wispy clouds. Oceanview Cove seemed to hold its breath under the soft lunar glow, its empty streets full of shadow and long stretches of moonlight. I stood on my porch, my heart hammering against my ribs as I surveyed the street.

Peter's house loomed before us, a dark silhouette against the star-speckled sky. Yellow police tape fluttered in the gentle sea breeze, an odd splash of color in the monochrome night. The windows, once warm and inviting, now stared back at me like vacant eyes, holding secrets I was desperate to uncover.

"Ready for this?" I whispered to Ginger, who sat perched on the railing, his tail twitching with anticipation.

"Born ready, old man," he replied, his green eyes glowing in the darkness. "Just try not to trip over your own feet while you're playing decoy."

I shot him a look, but there was no real heat in it. Truth be told, I was grateful for his cavalier attitude. It helped keep my nerves at bay.

We made our way down the street, our footsteps muffled by the soft grass. As we neared Peter's property, I could make out the figure of a police officer standing sentry near the front door. He looked bored, occasionally checking his watch in the dim glow of the porch light.

"Remember the plan," I murmured to Ginger. "I'll distract him while you sneak around back."

Ginger's whiskers twitched in what seemed like his version of a smirk. "Don't worry about me. Just make sure you keep Barney Fife over there occupied."

Before I could retort, Ginger had melted into the shadows, his orange fur blending seamlessly with the darkness. I took a deep breath, straightened my shoulders, and approached the officer.

"Evening, officer," I called out, trying to keep my voice steady.

The policeman startled, his hand instinctively moving to his hip before he recognized me. "Mr. Butterfield? What are you doing out so late?"

I forced a chuckle, hoping it didn't sound as nervous as I felt. "Couldn't sleep. Thought I'd take a walk, clear my head. This business with Peter, you know... it's weighing on me."

The officer's posture relaxed slightly, but I could see suspicion remaining in his eyes. "I can imagine. But you shouldn't be out here, sir. This is an active crime scene."

"Of course, of course," I nodded, taking a step closer. "I was just wondering... have you found anything new? Any leads?"

He shook his head, his expression a mixture of frustration and fatigue. "You know I can't discuss an ongoing investigation, Mr. Butterfield."

"Right, right," I said hurriedly. "It's just... Peter was my neighbor, you know? I can't help but wonder what happened to him."

As I rambled on, trying to keep the officer's attention, I silently prayed that Ginger was making progress inside the house. Suddenly, a loud meow echoed from within, causing both the officer and me to freeze.

"What a mess!" Ginger's voice rang out, though to the officer, it would have sounded like just a meow.

The officer frowned. "Did you hear that?"

I feigned confusion. "Hear what?"

Before the officer could respond, Ginger's voice came again. "I found something interesting!" Another meow to the officer's ears.

The policeman's suspicion visibly grew. "There it is again. Sounds like a cat."

"I didn't hear anything," I lied, my heart racing.

"Clear your ears, old man!" Ginger called out.

Without thinking, I responded, "Shush, I hear you."

The officer's eyebrows shot up. "Excuse me?"

Realizing my mistake, I scrambled to cover. "Oh, I... I was just talking to myself. Voices in my head, you know. Old age and living alone – quite the combination."

The officer's hand moved to his radio. "Mr. Butterfield, I think you should go home now."

Panic flared in my chest. Ginger needed more time. I launched into a rambling monologue about the importance of proper police procedure, peppering him with questions about protocol and chain of evidence. I was talking out of my hat, of course, cobbling together bits and pieces I'd gleaned from mystery novels over the years. But it seemed to be working. The officer looked increasingly flustered, clearly unsure how to handle this overly inquisitive old man.

Just when I was running out of law enforcement jargon to fumble through, I caught a flash of orange fur darting away from the back of Peter's house. A wave of relief washed over me. Ginger had made it out unseen, and now I could gracefully exit this increasingly awkward conversation.

"Well, I've taken up enough of your time," I said abruptly. "I should get back home."

The officer blinked, momentarily thrown by my sudden shift. "Uh, right. Yes, you should. And Mr. Butterfield?"

I paused, my heart in my throat. "Yes?"

"Please stay away from the crime scene from now on. For your own safety, you understand."

I nodded, not trusting myself to speak, and hurried back across the street. As soon as I was inside my own house, I sagged against the door, my legs suddenly weak.

"Nicely done, old man," Ginger's voice came from the darkness, making me jump. "I didn't think you had it in you to lie so convincingly."

"Yes, well," I muttered, fumbling for the light switch, "let's hope I never have to do it again. What did you find?"

As light flooded the room, I saw Ginger perched on the back of my armchair, looking immensely pleased with himself. "Oh," he purred. "Peter was hiding quite a few skeletons in his closet."

I sank into the chair, my heart still racing from our close call. "Tell me everything."

Ginger's tail swished back and forth as he began his report. "First things first. Peter's study was a mess, papers everywhere. But hidden behind a loose panel in his desk drawer, I found a stash of documents."

"What kind of documents?" I leaned forward, my fatigue forgotten in the face of this new development.

"Mostly property papers," Ginger said, his tail swishing thoughtfully. "And get this – there were records of some very large payments coming in."

I frowned, intrigued. "Payments? To or from Peter?"

"To Peter," Ginger clarified. "Substantial amounts, from what I could tell."

My mind raced with possibilities. "Could it be blackmail?"

Ginger shrugged, a surprisingly human gesture on a cat. "Possible. But that's not even the most interesting part. I found a letter, half-written. It was addressed to someone called 'M'."

"M?" I echoed. "Any idea who that could be?"

"No clue," Ginger admitted. "But whoever they are, Peter was planning something big with them. The letter said, 'We could go wherever you want...'"

I sat back, my head spinning. "So Peter was planning to leave town? With this mysterious 'M' person?"

"Looks that way," Ginger nodded. "And the fact that he hid the letter with those documents suggests it was a secret he was desperate to keep."

We sat in silence for a moment, the implications of this discovery settling over us like a heavy blanket. Suddenly, a thought struck me.

"Ginger," I said slowly, "what if 'M' stands for Maggie?"

Ginger's ears perked up. "The baker? You might be onto something there, old man. Peter and Maggie did have a history together, from what I've observed. Though Peter never brought her home and seemed to keep their relationship quiet."

I nodded, my mind racing. "That explains the secrecy. So they could be planning to leave town together..."

"We need to talk to her," Ginger said, his tail swishing with excitement. "First thing in the morning, we should head to the bakery."

I couldn't help but notice the gleam in Ginger's eye. "You just want another chance at those croissants, don't you?"

Ginger's whiskers twitched in amusement. "Can you blame me? They're delicious. Besides, a cat's got to eat, especially when he's helping solve a murder."

I chuckled, feeling a mix of anticipation and apprehension about our next move. As I prepared for bed, I couldn't shake the feeling that we were getting closer to the truth. But would that truth bring us clarity or only more questions?

***

The warm, inviting aroma of freshly baked bread and sweet pastries hung heavy in the air as I pushed open the door to Maggie's Bakery. The cheerful tinkle of the bell above the door seemed at odds with the knot of tension in my stomach. Ginger had reluctantly agreed to wait outside, grumbling about being persona non grata after an incident involving stolen croissants.

"You'd think they'd have forgotten by now," he'd muttered. "It was just one time... or maybe three."

The bakery was busy, as usual, but there was a subdued quality to the chatter that filled the air. It was as if the entire town was speaking in whispers, afraid to disturb the uneasy peace that had settled over Oceanview Cove in the wake of Peter's death.

Maggie stood behind the counter, her flour-dusted colorful apron highlighting her rosy face. She looked up as I approached, and I couldn't help but notice the dark circles under her eyes. Had she had those the last time I came here?

"Morning, Jim," she said, her smile not quite reaching her eyes. "How are you settling in? Can I get you something?"

I nodded, trying to keep my tone casual. "Morning, Maggie. I'm settling in fine, thanks. Could I get some of those delicious croissants again? They were a real treat last time."

"Of course," she replied, reaching for a paper bag. "How are you holding up? It's been a rough few days for the town. I bet this isn't quite the quiet retirement you had in mind when you moved here."

I hummed in agreement. "It's been quite the whirlwind, to put it mildly." I paused, watching her carefully as she selected my croissants. "I suppose everyone's still in shock about Peter. Such a terrible thing."

The paper bag slipped from Maggie's fingers, scattering croissants across the counter. "Oh! I'm so clumsy today," she exclaimed, her cheeks flushing as she scrambled to clean up the mess.

"Here, let me help," I offered, reaching for a fallen pastry.

"No, no, it's fine," Maggie insisted, her movements frantic as she swept the croissants into a bin behind the counter. "I'll get you fresh ones."

I watched as she bustled about, her usual grace replaced by a nervous energy that set my detective senses tingling. "Maggie," I said gently, "is everything alright?"

She paused, her back to me. For a moment, I thought she might ignore the question entirely. Then, with a deep breath, she turned to face me. "It's just... Peter's death. It's been hard on everyone."

I raised an eyebrow, trying to keep my expression neutral. "I see. Were you two close?"

Maggie's gaze dropped to the counter, her fingers idly tracing patterns in the scattered flour. "We had a... connection, once upon a time. It was brief, but quite hard to forget. That was years ago, though."

I nodded, considering my next words carefully. "You know," I said, keeping my voice light. "I was chatting with the police officer outside Peter's house yesterday, and he mentioned something about a letter they found. Half-written, addressed to someone with the initial 'M'."

The color drained from Maggie's face so quickly I thought she might faint. "A letter?" she repeated, her voice barely above a whisper.

I nodded, watching her reaction closely. "Apparently, it seemed like Peter was planning a trip with someone. I thought maybe you might know something about it."

Maggie's hands gripped the edge of the counter, her knuckles white. "I... I don't know anything about that," she said, but her eyes darted away from mine, unable to hold my gaze.

"Are you sure, Maggie?" I pressed gently. "If you know anything that might help us understand what happened to him..."

"There's nothing to tell," Maggie snapped, her voice sharper than I'd ever heard it. Then, as if realizing how she sounded, she softened her tone. "I'm sorry, Jim. It's just... this has all been so overwhelming. Peter and I, we were in the past. So whatever he was planning, whoever he was writing to, it wasn't me."

I held up my hands in a placating gesture. "Of course. I'm sorry if I upset you, Maggie. I'm just trying to make sense of everything."

Maggie nodded, visibly composing herself. "I understand. Here," she said, handing me a fresh bag of croissants. "I hope you find the answers you're looking for."

There was a finality in her tone that told me our conversation was over. I thanked her and made my way to the door, my mind whirling with new questions and suspicions.

As I stepped out into the bright morning sunlight, Ginger materialized at my feet, his nose twitching eagerly. "Well?" he demanded. "What did you find out? And more importantly, where are my croissants?"

I glanced around to make sure no one was within earshot before responding. "Maggie and Peter did have a history together, just like you said," I murmured, bending down to pretend I was petting Ginger as I spoke. "She claims it was all in the past, but her reaction when I mentioned the letter... Ginger, I think she's hiding something."

Ginger's tail swished thoughtfully. "So our sweet baker might have a sour secret. Interesting. Did she admit to being the mysterious 'M'?"

I shook my head. "She denied it outright. But you should have seen her face when I brought it up. She looked terrified."

"Maybe she was just shocked that you were poking your nose into Peter's affairs," Ginger suggested, his tone dry.

I winced. "Yes, well, I may have implied that I heard it from the police. Not my proudest moment, I'll admit."

Ginger snorted. "Look at you, old man. Fibbing to sweet ladies. You're turning into a regular criminal mastermind."

I felt a flush of shame creep up my neck. "It's not like that. I'm just trying to get to the truth."

"And the truth is getting more complicated by the minute," Ginger observed. "So, what's our next move, Watson?"

I sighed, running a hand through my thinning hair. "I'm not sure. Maggie's definitely hiding something, but I don't think she's our killer. If anything, she seemed genuinely upset about Peter's death."

As we started to walk away from the bakery, a thought struck me. "You know, we should probably talk to Ryan. He seems to know everything about everyone in this town. Maybe he's heard some gossip that could help us."

Ginger's ears perked up. "The nosy neighbor with the newspaper? Not a bad idea. We should swing by the newspaper office. He's likely to be there at this time of the day."

I nodded. "You're right. And in all the excitement, I completely forgot about wanting to apologize to him for being grumpy the other night. With any luck, we might kill two birds with one stone – smooth things over with Ryan and get some useful information."

Chapter 10

The Oceanview Cove Gazette office stood at the corner of Main Street and Harbor Lane, an old two-story building that had clearly seen better days. The faded blue paint was peeling in places, revealing the worn wood beneath, and the brass nameplate beside the door had long since lost its shine. Yet there was a certain charm to the place, a sense of history and importance that seemed to radiate from its very foundations.

As Ginger and I approached, I couldn't help but feel a mix of anticipation and nervousness. Ryan had always struck me as a bit of a busybody, but right now, his penchant for gossip might be exactly what we needed.

"Remember," Ginger muttered as we neared the entrance, "play it cool. We're just here for a friendly chat, not an interrogation."

I nodded, taking a deep breath before pushing open the heavy wooden door. A small bell jingled overhead, announcing our arrival.

The interior of the Gazette office was completely different from its somewhat outdated exterior. The space was surprisingly bright and airy, with large windows letting in plenty of natural light. The walls were covered in framed newspaper clippings, chronicling decades of Oceanview Cove's history. The air was thick with the scent of ink and paper, underlined by the faint aroma of coffee.

To our left, a cluttered reception area housed a desk piled high with papers, an ancient-looking computer, and a potted plant that had seen better days. To our right, several desks were arranged in a haphazard pattern, each one a small island of organized chaos. The steady clack-clack of computer keyboards filled the air, punctuated by the occasional ring of a telephone.

A young woman with bright red hair looked up from the reception desk as we entered. Her eyes widened slightly at the sight of Ginger, but she quickly composed herself.

"Can I help you?" she asked, her voice friendly but with an undercurrent of curiosity.

"Yes, I'm looking for Ryan Perkins," I replied, trying to sound casual. "Is he in?"

The woman nodded, gesturing towards the back of the office. "He's in his office. Just head straight back, you can't miss it."

I thanked her and headed towards the rear of the building, Ginger beside me. As we walked, I couldn't help but marvel at the organized chaos around us. Every available surface seemed to be covered in papers, notebooks, or bits of technology. A large cork board dominated one wall, covered in a dizzying array of post-it notes, photographs, and scraps of paper connected by colorful strings. It looked like something out of a detective movie.

"Quite the operation they've got here," Ginger murmured, his eyes darting around the room. "I bet old Ryan's got dirt on everyone in town squirreled away somewhere."

I hushed him as we approached a door at the back of the room. A brass plaque declared it to be the office of "Ryan Perkins, Editor-in-Chief." I took another deep breath, steeling myself, and knocked.

"Come in!" Ryan's voice called from inside.

I pushed open the door, Ginger slipping in behind me before I could stop him. Ryan's office was a microcosm of the larger newsroom – every surface was covered in papers, books, and various knick-knacks. The man himself sat behind a large, antique desk, peering at us over the top of his wire-rimmed glasses.

"Jim!" Ryan exclaimed, his face breaking into a wide smile. "What a pleasant surprise!" His eyes then fell on Ginger, curiosity flickering across his face. "And Ginger? I'm surprised to see you here. Following Jim around now, are you?"

"He seems to have taken a liking to me," I said. Then, feeling I should elaborate, I added, "After Peter's passing, I decided to look after Ginger. It felt like the right thing to do."

Ryan's expression softened, a shadow of sadness passing over his features. "Ah, yes. Peter's death... it's still hard to believe he's gone." Ryan shook his head slightly, as if to clear away the somber thoughts. "Well, have a seat, both of you! What brings you to the hallowed halls of the Oceanview Cove Gazette?"

I settled into one of the chairs facing Ryan's desk, while Ginger made himself comfortable on a stack of old newspapers. "Well, Ryan," I began, "I actually wanted to apologize for the other night. When I left Peter's house, I wasn't very friendly. I was upset, and I took it out on you. That wasn't fair."

Ryan waved a hand dismissively. "Water under the bridge, my friend. These are trying times for all of us. I completely understand."

I nodded, relieved that he wasn't holding a grudge. "Thank you. And speaking of trying times... I was hoping I could ask you a few questions about what happened that night. You see, I've been trying to piece things together, to understand what happened to Peter."

Ryan leaned back in his chair, his expression turning serious. "Of course, of course. Terrible business, that. I'm actually working on a piece about it for our next edition. What would you like to know?"

I decided to start with something simple. "Well, you saw me leaving Peter's house that night. Did you notice anything unusual? Anyone else coming or going?"

Ryan's brow furrowed in concentration. "Let me think... No, I don't believe so. It was a quiet night, as I recall. You left Peter's house looking quite upset, and that was about it."

I nodded, trying to keep my expression neutral. "And what about earlier in the evening? Did you see Peter with anyone?"

"Hmm..." Ryan tapped his chin thoughtfully. "No, I can't say that I did. Peter kept to himself most days."

I decided to take a chance. "What about Maggie? I heard she and Peter were close."

Ryan's eyebrows shot up. "Oh? Yes, they go way back. Used to be quite the item years ago, if you know what I mean." He winked conspiratorially.

"Subtle as a brick through a window, this one," Ginger muttered sarcastically.

I feigned surprise, carefully concealing the fact that Maggie had already told me about her past with Peter. This was an opportunity to gather more information, and I didn't want to show my hand too soon. "Really? Maggie didn't mention that when I talked to her earlier."

Ryan's expression flickered for a moment. "Oh? Well, I suppose it was a long time ago. Ancient history and all that."

Something in his tone made me pause. He seemed almost... too casual about it. I decided to press a little harder. "Ryan, in your opinion, is there any chance that Maggie might have had something to do with Peter's death?"

Ryan's reaction was immediate and emphatic. "Maggie? Good heavens, no! She's the sweetest soul in Oceanview Cove. Wouldn't hurt a fly, that one."

"No, she'd just thrash it with a rolling pin," Ginger quipped under his breath.

I held up my hands in a calming gesture. "Of course, I'm not suggesting anything. I'm just trying to understand all the relationships at play here."

Ryan nodded, but I noticed a slight tightness around his eyes. "Understandable, of course. But really, Jim, I think you're barking up the wrong tree there. Maggie and Peter were friends, nothing more."

I frowned slightly. "But you just said they used to be an item?"

"Ah, well," Ryan backpedaled, "that was years ago. Ancient history, like I said."

Ginger chose that moment to leap onto Ryan's desk, scattering papers everywhere.

"Oh, I'm so sorry!" I exclaimed, jumping up to grab the cat. As I leaned across the desk, I caught a glimpse of a notepad partially hidden under a stack of files. The name "Maggie" was scrawled across the top, followed by what looked like a list of times and dates.

Ryan quickly swept the notepad out of sight, laughing nervously. "No harm done! Cats will be cats, eh?"

"Some of us more than others," Ginger said, looking entirely too pleased with himself.

I nodded, my mind whirling. What was on that notepad? And why was Ryan so quick to hide it?

As I settled back into my chair, I decided to try a different tack. "Ryan, you seem to know everyone in town.

In your opinion, was there anyone who might have had a reason to want to harm Peter?"

Ryan's expression turned thoughtful. "Well, I've heard some talk about Peter being involved in property dealings down at the docks that weren't exactly popular with everyone, especially with Reeves. He didn't like it much, from what I gathered. But I don't know the details, mind you. Just bits and pieces I've picked up around town."

I leaned forward, intrigued. "Robert Reeves? The fisherman?"

Ryan nodded. "The very same. But listen, Jim, there's something else you should know. I heard some chatter near the police station. They say they've found evidence against you."

"Evidence? You mean the fingerprints on the beer bottle? I already know about those."

Ryan shook his head, lowering his voice. "No, it's more than that. I don't know the specifics, but word is they've found something new. Something big."

My heart sank at this news. New evidence? What could they possibly have found? I wracked my brain, trying to think of anything I might have overlooked, any detail that could incriminate me. But I came up blank. The fact that I was innocent should have been reassuring, but instead, it made me feel even more vulnerable. If they could find evidence against an innocent man, what else might they "discover"?

I must have paled visibly, because Ryan leaned forward, concern etched on his face. "You alright there, Jim?"

I nodded, trying to compose myself. "Yes, I'm... I'm fine. Just surprised, that's all." I took a deep breath, attempting to steady my nerves. This was troubling news, and it only added to the growing unease I'd been feeling. But something still felt off. Ryan was being helpful, almost too helpful, yet there was a nervous edge to his manner when Maggie's name came up.

"Ryan," I said slowly, choosing my words carefully, my voice sounding strained even to my own ears, "I appreciate all this information. But I can't shake the feeling that there's something you're not telling me. Especially about Maggie."

Ryan's friendly demeanor faltered for a moment, a flash of fear crossing his face before he composed himself. "I'm not sure what you mean, Jim. I've told you everything I know. There's nothing more to it."

I studied Ryan's face, searching for any hint of the truth he might be hiding. But his expression had closed off, and I realized that pushing further would likely only make him more defensive. It seemed I had reached the limits of what he was willing to share, at least for now.

I stood up, deciding it was time to end our conversation. "Well, thank you for your time, Ryan. You've been very helpful."

Ryan looked relieved as he showed us to the door. "Any time, Jim. And please, don't hesitate to come by if you have any more questions. We at the Gazette are always happy to help our fellow citizens."

As Ginger and I stepped out into the bright sunlight, I felt a mix of frustration and excitement. We'd learned some new information, but we'd also uncovered what seemed to be a whole new layer of secrets.

"Well," Ginger said as we started walking back towards my house, "that was about as illuminating as a burned-out lightbulb."

I nodded, still lost in thought. "Ryan's definitely hiding something. But what? And why?"

Ginger's tail swished thoughtfully. "Maybe he's sweet on the baker? Wouldn't be the first time a man did something stupid for love."

I couldn't help but chuckle at that. "You might be right. But where does that leave us? We seem to have more questions than answers." Then, remembering Ryan's troubling news, I added, "And what about this new evidence the police supposedly found? That's got me worried, Ginger. What could they possibly have discovered?"

Ginger flicked his ear dismissively. "Don't let it rattle you, old man. If you're innocent, which I know you are, they can't have found anything real."

As we walked, I couldn't shake the feeling that we were missing something important. The pieces were all there – Peter's secret documents, the mysterious letter, Maggie's evasiveness, Ryan's contradictions – but I couldn't quite see how they fit together.

Suddenly, Ginger stopped in his tracks, his ears perking up. "You know, old man, I just had a thought. Ryan's at work now, right?"

I nodded, not sure where he was going with this. "Yes, why?"

Ginger's whiskers twitched in what seemed like a mischievous grin. "Well, if he's at work, that means his house is empty. And if I were a betting cat, I'd wager there are plenty of interesting things to be found there."

I felt a mixture of shock and excitement at the suggestion. "Ginger, are you proposing we break into Ryan's house?"

"Break in is such a harsh term," Ginger purred. "I prefer to think of it as... an unauthorized fact-finding mission."

Ginger had a point. With the fingerprints on the beer bottle and this mysterious new evidence Ryan had mentioned, the police seemed to be building a case against me. It was only a matter of time before Sheriff Miller hauled me in for a more intense interrogation, or worse, took me into custody. The thought sent a chill down my spine. We needed to gather more information, and quickly, if I was going to clear my name. As much as the idea of snooping made me uncomfortable, I was running out of options.

***

I took a deep breath, my heart pounding in my chest as I watched Ginger slink towards Ryan's house. The cat moved with a grace and stealth that I couldn't help but envy, especially considering what we were about to do.

"Keep an eye out," Ginger instructed.

With that, he darted across the lawn and disappeared around the side of the house. I stood there, feeling exposed and more than a little foolish, as I waited for what felt like an eternity. Finally, I heard a soft thud from the back of the house.

"Coast is clear, old man," Ginger's voice drifted to me. "Window's open. Try not to make too much noise coming in."

I made my way around to the back, where I found a ground-floor window pushed slightly ajar. Taking one last look around to ensure no one was watching, I gripped the windowsill and started to hoist myself up.

It was immediately apparent that this was going to be more challenging than I'd anticipated. I grunted with effort, my arms straining as I tried to pull my less-than-athletic body through the narrow opening.

"Having trouble there, Jim?" Ginger's amused voice came from inside. "Maybe lay off the croissants for a while, eh?"

"Very funny," I gasped, finally managing to squeeze through. I tumbled unceremoniously onto the floor, landing in an undignified heap. "I really need to start exercising more."

As I picked myself up, dusting off my clothes, I took in my surroundings. Ryan's house was surprisingly neat and orderly, a stark contrast to the chaotic newspaper office. The furniture was modern and minimalist, with everything arranged just so. It felt almost too perfect, like a showroom rather than a lived-in home.

"Well, this is unexpected," I murmured. "Not quite what I imagined."

Ginger nodded, his tail swishing thoughtfully. "It's like he's got a split personality. Chaos at work, perfect order at home."

"Where should we start?" I asked, still feeling uneasy about the whole situation.

"You take the living room and kitchen," Ginger instructed. "I'll check out the bedroom and study. And remember, we're looking for anything related to Peter or Maggie."

I nodded, watching as Ginger walked silently out of the room. Taking a deep breath, I began my search. The living room yielded nothing of interest – just a few generic decorative items and a well-organized bookshelf filled with true crime novels and history books.

The kitchen was equally unremarkable. I rifled through drawers and cupboards, feeling increasingly guilty with each invasion of privacy. Just as I was about to give up and check on Ginger's progress, something caught my eye. A small notepad was tucked behind the microwave, partially hidden from view.

I pulled it out and flipped it open, my heart racing. The first page was filled with what looked like a shopping list, but as I turned the pages, I found something far more interesting. Ryan had been keeping notes on his neighbors – detailed observations about their comings and goings, their habits, even snippets of overheard conversations.

"Ginger," I called softly. "I think I've found something."

The cat appeared in the doorway, his green eyes gleaming with interest. "What is it?"

I held up the notepad. "Looks like our friendly neighborhood journalist has been doing some extracurricular reporting."

Ginger leapt onto the counter for a closer look. "Well, well. Seems like Ryan's nosiness goes beyond his professional life. Anything about Peter or Maggie in there?"

I flipped through the pages, scanning quickly. "Yes, here's something about Peter... 'Met with unknown man in town square, seemed agitated.' And Maggie... 'Peter visited bakery late evening, left looking upset.'" I looked up at Ginger, my brow furrowed. "But it's all just observations. There's nothing here that directly ties Ryan to Peter's murder."

I continued to flip through the pages, and suddenly, I noticed my own name. "Well, would you look at that," I muttered. "He's even got notes about me. 'New neighbor Jim – retired librarian. Talks to Peter's cat. Possible early signs of dementia? Keep an eye on him.'"

I couldn't help but feel a mix of amusement and indignation. "Early signs of dementia? I guess he was mad at me for what I said the other night. Though I suppose talking to a cat might not help my case," I added with a wry smile.

Ginger's whiskers twitched. "Well, he's not entirely wrong about keeping an eye on you, is he? Though I'd argue it's your newfound penchant for breaking and entering that's more concerning than any supposed dementia."

"I was hoping for something more concrete," I sighed, closing the notebook. "Did you find anything interesting in the bedroom or study?"

Ginger shook his head. "Nothing that points to Peter and Maggie."

Before I could respond, we both froze at the sound of a key turning in the front door lock.

Panic surged through me. "Ryan," I whispered, my eyes darting around frantically for an escape route. "He must be home early."

Chapter 11

The sound of the front door opening sent a jolt of panic through my entire body. I froze, the notepad still clutched in my trembling hands, as Ryan's footsteps echoed through the house.

"Hide!" Ginger hissed, already darting towards the kitchen door.

I didn't need to be told twice. Adrenaline surging, I scrambled after Ginger, my heart pounding so loudly I was sure Ryan would hear it. We slipped into the hallway just as Ryan's keys clattered onto the table in the living room.

"Hello?" Ryan called out. "Is someone there?"

I pressed myself against the wall, hardly daring to breathe. Ginger, the traitor, had already disappeared around the corner, leaving me alone with my panic and the incriminating notepad.

Ryan's footsteps grew closer. I inched along the wall, desperately searching for an escape route. The bathroom door was ajar just a few feet away. It was a risk, but I had no choice. I slipped inside just as Ryan rounded the corner.

"Huh," I heard him mutter. "Could've sworn I heard something."

I leaned against the bathroom door, my chest heaving. This was not how I'd envisioned spending my retirement. Breaking and entering, hiding in bathrooms – what would Martha think of me now?

A soft meow from outside the door nearly made me jump out of my skin. Ginger! The blasted cat was going to get us caught!

"Oh, it's Peter's... now Jim's cat," Ryan's voice said, surprise evident in his tone. "Ginger, how did you get in here?" There was a pause, then a sigh. "I should've sealed up that pet flap ages ago."

I held my breath, waiting for the moment Ryan would realize something was amiss. But to my immense relief, Ginger played his part perfectly, letting out another soft meow.

"Are you hungry? Let me see if I have any tuna for you."

Ryan's footsteps retreated towards the kitchen. I cracked open the bathroom door, peering out cautiously. The coast was clear. Now was our chance.

I tiptoed down the hallway, Ginger materializing at my side. "Nice distraction," I whispered.

"Amateur," Ginger replied. "Now let's get out of here before he comes back with that tuna. It's probably some cheap, off-brand stuff anyway."

We made our way back to the living room, our exit so close I could almost taste freedom. I hastily placed the notebook where I'd found it, hoping Ryan wouldn't notice it had been disturbed. But as I approached the window, a new problem presented itself. Getting in had been a challenge – getting out might prove impossible.

"Um, Ginger?" I whispered, eyeing the window. "I'm not sure I can—"

"Oh, for Pete's sake," Ginger grumbled. "Just start climbing. I'll help push."

With a deep breath, I hoisted myself onto the windowsill. It was a tight squeeze, and for a moment, I was certain I'd be stuck there forever, half in and half out of Ryan's house like some bizarre home decoration.

"Hurry up!" Ginger hissed. "He'll be back any second!"

I wiggled and squirmed, trying to force my way through the narrow opening. Just when I thought all hope was lost, I felt a pressure against my rear. Ginger was pushing me with all his might.

"This is undignified," I grunted.

"Less talking, more wiggling," Ginger retorted.

With one final push from Ginger and a desperate lunge on my part, I tumbled out of the window, landing on Ryan's lawn.

Ginger leapt out after me, landing with far more grace than I could ever hope to achieve. "Well," he said, looking down at me, "that was about as subtle as a herd of elephants in a china shop."

I picked myself up, brushing dirt from my clothes. "Let's just get out of here before—"

"Ginger? Where are you?"

Ryan's voice drifted from the open window, sending a fresh wave of panic through me. Without a word, Ginger and I took off, sprinting across Ryan's lawn and down the street. We didn't stop until we were safely back in my house, the door locked firmly behind us.

I collapsed into my armchair, my lungs burning and my heart racing. "That," I gasped, "was far too close for comfort."

Ginger, looking annoyingly unruffled, hopped onto the coffee table. "On the bright side, we didn't get caught. And we did find something interesting."

I nodded, still trying to catch my breath. "Yes, but what does it mean? All these observations about the townspeople – it's odd, certainly, but does it connect to Peter's murder?"

Ginger's tail swished thoughtfully. "Maybe not directly, but it does show that Ryan's got his nose in everyone's business. And he's clearly been keeping tabs on both Peter and Maggie."

I frowned, recalling the contents of the notebook. "There's got to be more to it than just nosy neighbor syndrome. Ryan seemed awfully quick to defend Maggie earlier. And now we find out he's been watching her closely?"

"Not to mention his notes about Peter meeting someone in the town square," Ginger added. "That could be important."

I nodded, an idea forming. "You know, we've been so focused on Maggie, we might be missing something. What if we're looking at this all wrong?"

Ginger cocked his head. "What do you mean?"

"Well, think about it. Everyone in town seems to have some connection to Peter. What if the key isn't in his personal relationships, but in his business dealings?"

"The property dealings Ryan mentioned and the papers I found in Peter's study," Ginger said, his eyes lighting up with understanding.

"Exactly," I said, feeling a surge of excitement. "Peter was involved in some kind of deal down at the docks. Robert Reeves wasn't happy about it. And now Peter's dead."

Ginger nodded slowly. "It's worth looking into. But how do we find out more? It's not like we can go asking Robert Reeves – he'd probably throw you into the harbor if you showed up again."

I leaned back in my chair, considering our options. Then it hit me. "Shawn," I said. "The bartender at the Salty Breeze. He seems to know everything that goes on in this town. And he was friendly towards me last time."

"Plus, I could probably listen in on some more gossip while we're there," Ginger added.

I nodded, glancing at the clock. "Good idea, but it's still a few hours before the evening crowd will be there. I think I'll take a brief nap first. This amateur sleuthing is more tiring than I expected."

As I stood up, ready to head to the bedroom, I caught sight of myself in the mirror. My clothes were rumpled and dirt-stained, my hair a wild mess. I looked less like a respectable retiree and more like someone who'd just wrestled with an unruly lawn mower.

"Maybe a quick change of clothes first," I muttered.

Ginger snickered. "Probably for the best. You look like you've been dragged through a hedge backwards. Which, come to think of it, isn't far from the truth."

***

After a brief nap on the living room couch it was time to freshen up. I headed to the bedroom and opened my wardrobe. Opting for a casual but respectable outfit that wouldn't look out of place at the Salty Breeze, I chose a comfortable pair of khakis and a light blue button-down shirt, topped with a navy blazer. As I emerged from the bedroom, now dressed and ready, Ginger eyed me critically.

"Not bad, old man," he said. "You almost look like you belong in this century."

I rolled my eyes. "Come on, you furry critic. Let's go see what Shawn knows."

As we approached the Salty Breeze, Ginger darted ahead. "I'll sneak in through that open window and keep an ear out for any gossip," he said. "You just focus on Shawn."

I pushed open the door to the Salty Breeze, the familiar scent of stale beer and old wood enveloping me like a well-worn jacket. The bar was quieter than usual, with only a handful of patrons scattered about, nursing their drinks in contemplative silence. Shawn stood behind the bar, polishing a glass with the absent-minded dedication of a man who'd performed the task a thousand times before.

As I approached, Shawn's face broke into a smile. "Jim! Back so soon? Don't tell me you've already developed a taste for my special concoctions."

I chuckled, settling onto a barstool. "Not quite, Shawn. Though I wouldn't say no to another of those Librarian cocktails."

Shawn's eyes twinkled as he set about mixing the drink. "So, what brings you back to my humble establishment? More questions about our dearly departed Peter, I'd wager?"

I nodded, accepting the glass Shawn slid towards me. "You've got me pegged, Shawn. I was hoping you might be able to shed some light on Peter's... business dealings."

Shawn's bushy eyebrows rose slightly. "Business dealings, eh? That's a can of worms you're looking to open there, Jim."

I took a sip of my drink, savoring the complex flavors. "I've heard some talk about property deals. Thought you might know something about that."

Shawn glanced around the bar, then leaned in closer, his voice dropping to a conspiratorial whisper. "Well, since you're asking... Peter had been in talks with some hotshot developer from the city. Wanted to sell his house, if you can believe it."

So that's what those ownership papers and payments in Peter's house were about. "Sell his house? But why? It seemed like such a lovely place."

Shawn nodded, his expression grim. "Oh, it was. But this developer, he had big plans. Wanted to turn it into one of those fancy bed and breakfast places."

I whistled low. "I can't imagine that went over well with the neighbors."

"Like a lead balloon," Shawn confirmed. "Folks around here, they value their peace and quiet. The idea of having a flow of tourists next door... well, it didn't sit right with most."

I took another sip of my drink, mulling over this information. "I can see why. But surely Peter knew how unpopular this would be. Why go through with it?"

Shawn shrugged, reaching for another glass to polish. "Money talks, Jim. And from what I heard, this developer was offering a pretty penny. But if you ask me, there was more to it than that. Peter seemed... anxious about the whole thing. Like he was being pushed into it, somehow."

My ears perked up at this. "Pushed? By whom?"

"That, I don't know," he said, shaking his head. "But in the weeks leading up to his death, Peter was different. He'd come in here, order his usual, but his eyes would dart around like he was expecting trouble. He'd check his phone constantly, jump at sudden noises. It wasn't like him at all. Peter was always a laid-back kind of guy, you know? Seeing him so on edge... it was unsettling."

I nodded, filing this information away. "What about other property dealings? I'd heard something about Peter being involved in some deal down at the docks?"

Shawn's brow furrowed. "The docks? Can't say I've heard anything about that. Where'd you pick that up?"

I hesitated, catching myself before I revealed too much. "Oh, just something I picked up here and there," I said, aiming for a casual tone. "You know how people talk in a small town. I wasn't sure if there was any truth to it."

Shawn nodded, though I could see a flicker of suspicion in his eyes. "Well, if there was something going on down at the docks, it's news to me. But then again, Peter always did play things close to the chest."

I finished my drink, my mind whirling with this new information. "Thanks, Shawn. You've been a big help."

"Jim?" Shawn called out as I stood to leave. He leaned in, lowering his voice. "Be careful, yeah? Peter was a good man, but it seems like he got mixed up in something nasty. I'd hate to see the same happen to you."

I nodded, touched by his concern. "I appreciate that, Shawn. I'll watch my step."

As I went outside into the cool evening air, Ginger materialized beside me. "Well?" he asked, his tail twitching impatiently. "What did our friendly neighborhood barkeep have to say?"

I filled Ginger in on my conversation with Shawn as we walked. In return, Ginger shared some of the gossip he'd overheard. "Old man Jenkins is convinced the town council is secretly run by the aliens," he snickered. "And apparently, the postman thinks the weather's been unusually good lately because of government experiments with cloud seeding."

I chuckled, shaking my head. "Any useful information?"

Ginger's whiskers twitched. "No, you know how people can be after a few drinks. More wild theories than useful facts."

As we rounded the corner onto our street, I stopped short. There, parked in front of my house, was a police cruiser. Sheriff Miller stood on my front porch, his expression grim.

"Oh, this can't be good," Ginger muttered.

I approached cautiously, my heart pounding. "Evening, Sheriff," I called out, trying to keep my voice steady. "What brings you to our neighborhood?"

Miller turned to face me, his eyes hard. "Mr. Butterfield. I'm afraid I'm going to need you to come down to the station with me. We've got some evidence we need to discuss."

I felt a chill run down my spine. "Evidence? What kind of evidence?"

Miller held up a clear plastic bag containing a familiar-looking beer bottle. "We've finished processing the fingerprints from the night of Peter's murder. Your prints are all over this bottle, Mr. Butterfield."

I couldn't help but let out a dry chuckle. "Why did it take you so long to identify them? I told you they're mine. I had a beer with Peter that night, remember?"

Miller's eyes narrowed. "Be that as it may, we've also uncovered something else. Something that casts your involvement in a whole new light."

Miller produced another evidence bag. Inside was a neatly folded handkerchief. My eyes widened as I recognized the delicate embroidery spelling out "Butterfield" – the handiwork of my late wife, Martha.

"We found this in the trash can in front of your house," Miller said, his voice stern. "It has traces of the poison that killed Peter Johnson on it. Is this your handkerchief?"

My mind reeled. How could my handkerchief have ended up there? "Yes, but where... where exactly did you find that?" I stammered.

"As I said, in your trash can out front," Miller repeated.

I frowned, a spark of indignation cutting through my shock. "Isn't that a violation of my privacy? How could you search my trash without my permission?"

Miller's expression remained impassive. "Mr. Butterfield, under the law, trash left out for collection is considered abandoned property. Once it's placed in a public area for pickup, it's no longer protected by the Fourth Amendment. We didn't need a warrant to search it."

I stood there, stunned into silence. The implications of what Miller was saying slowly sank in.

"Now," Miller continued, "I'm going to need you to come down to the station for some additional questioning. Will you come quietly, or do I need to make this official?"

Realizing I had no choice, I nodded slowly. "I'll come," I said, my voice barely above a whisper.

As Miller led me to his patrol car, I caught a glimpse of an orange blur darting into the shadows. Ginger. I could only hope that my feline partner would find a way to continue our investigation while I was detained at the station.

Settling into the back of the police car, I couldn't help but wonder how my quiet retirement had turned into this surreal nightmare. As we pulled away from the curb, I saw Ryan peeking out from behind his curtains. No doubt he was already planning how to spin this latest development for his newspaper.

I leaned my head against the cool glass of the window, watching my newfound home fade into the distance. The weight of Martha's embroidered handkerchief pressed heavily on my mind. Someone wanted to set me up, but I knew the truth: I was innocent. Now I just had to figure out how to prove it – preferably before I ended up as the star attraction in a small-town murder trial.

Chapter 12

As Sheriff Miller's cruiser wound its way through the quiet streets of Oceanview Cove, my mind raced. The handkerchief – how could I have been so careless? I wracked my brain, trying to retrace my steps over the past few days. Where could I have lost it? And more importantly, who would want to use it to frame me?

I thought back to my visit to the docks, where I'd confronted the gruff Robert Reeves. Had I taken out my handkerchief then, perhaps to wipe the sweat off my forehead after that intense conversation? Could Reeves have somehow gotten hold of it during our tense exchange? The man certainly had motive, given his argument with Peter a few days before Peter's death.

Then there was Maggie's bakery, with its warm aromas and delicious pastries. I'd used my handkerchief there, hadn't I? To dab at a bit of croissant crumb on my chin. Maggie had been acting strangely, evasive about her relationship with Peter. Could the sweet-faced baker be harboring darker motives?

The Salty Breeze came to mind next, Shawn's knowing eyes and carefully chosen words suddenly seeming more suspicious. Had I left the handkerchief on the bar, distracted by our conversation about Peter's secrets? Shawn seemed to know an awful lot about the goings-on in town. Perhaps he knew more than he was letting on.

And what about Ryan? His notepad full of observations suddenly seemed far more ominous. I'd been so focused on not getting caught during our break-in that I might have dropped the handkerchief without noticing. And Ryan's contradictory statements at the Gazette office – could he be more involved than he let on?

Even Emma, the eccentric astrologer, flitted through my mind. She'd been so insistent about danger coming my way. Could her warnings have been more than just vague predictions? But no, that seemed too far-fetched, even in this town of secrets.

Round and round my suspicions went, like a carousel of potential culprits, each as unlikely as the next. By the time we pulled up to the police station, my head was spinning, and I was no closer to an answer.

The Oceanview Cove police station was a squat, unassuming building that looked more like an oversized beach house than a center of law enforcement. Its weathered clapboard exterior and faded blue paint job did little to inspire confidence in the town's criminal justice system. As Miller led me inside, I couldn't help but wonder if the laid-back appearance extended to their investigative skills as well.

We passed through a small reception area, where a bored-looking officer barely glanced up from her crossword puzzle as we entered. The interior was a maze of cramped hallways and cluttered desks, the air heavy with the scent of stale coffee and photocopier toner.

Miller steered me towards a door at the end of the hallway. As he pushed it open, I was hit with a wave of cool air and the harsh glare of fluorescent lighting. The interrogation room was small and claustrophobic, its walls a dingy shade of off-white that seemed designed to sap the spirit of anyone unfortunate enough to find themselves within.

"Have a seat, Mr. Butterfield," Miller said, gesturing to one of the two chairs flanking a battered metal table. I lowered myself into the seat, the chair creaking ominously under my weight.

Miller took the seat opposite me, his face an unreadable mask. He placed a file folder on the table between us, its contents a mystery that made my stomach churn with anxiety.

"Now then," he began, his voice deceptively calm, "why don't we start at the beginning? Tell me again about the night Peter died."

I took a deep breath, willing my voice to remain steady. "As I've told you before, Sheriff, I went over to Peter's house for a beer. We chatted for a while, and then I left. That's all there is to it."

Miller nodded slowly, his eyes never leaving my face. "And you're certain that's everything? Nothing else happened that night?"

"Nothing," I insisted. "We had a beer, we talked, and I went home. I didn't even know anything had happened to him until the next day."

Miller leaned back in his chair, looking at me with a mixture of skepticism and something that might have been disappointment. "Mr. Butterfield, I want to believe you. I really do. But the evidence we've uncovered... it's not looking good for you. Let's talk about that handkerchief, shall we?"

I swallowed hard, trying to keep my voice steady. "What about it, Sheriff?"

Miller's eyes narrowed. "You claim it's yours, correct?"

I nodded. "Yes, it is. I must have misplaced it a few days ago. I had no idea where it had gone."

"A few days ago," Miller repeated, his tone skeptical. "That's awfully convenient timing, don't you think? Just happened to lose it right around the time Peter was murdered."

I felt a bead of sweat trickle down my temple. "It's the truth, Sheriff. I'm an old man, I lose things all the time."

Miller leaned forward, his voice taking on a harder edge. "Mr. Butterfield, do you expect me to believe that you just happened to lose a handkerchief, which then just happened to end up in your trash can, covered in the same poison that killed your neighbor? That's quite a coincidence, don't you think?"

I took a deep breath, trying to stay calm. "I know how it looks, Sheriff. But I'm telling you, I had nothing to do with Peter's death. Someone must be trying to frame me."

Miller's eyebrows shot up. "Frame you? That's a serious accusation, Mr. Butterfield. Do you have any idea who might want to do that? Any enemies in town?"

I hesitated, knowing how ridiculous my suspicions would sound. "I... I'm not sure. I've only been in town a short while. But there are people who might have had reasons to want Peter dead."

"Oh?" Miller's interest perked up. "And who might those people be?"

I opened my mouth, then closed it again. How could I explain my suspicions without revealing the extent of my amateur sleuthing? "Well, there's Robert Reeves," I said finally. "I heard he and Peter had some kind of argument a few days before Peter's death."

Miller nodded slowly. "We're aware of their disagreement. Anyone else?"

I thought of Maggie, of Ryan, of Shawn. But I had no real evidence against any of them, just hunches and half-formed theories. "No one I can say for certain," I admitted.

Miller's expression hardened. "Mr. Butterfield, I've been doing this job for a long time. And in my experience, innocent men don't usually find themselves in situations like this. They certainly don't have poison-laced handkerchiefs showing up in their trash."

I felt a surge of indignation. "With all due respect, Sheriff, I've never been in a situation like this before. I'm an innocent man, and I'm telling you the truth!"

"The truth?" Miller's voice rose slightly. "The truth is that all the evidence points to you, Mr. Butterfield. Your fingerprints on the beer bottle at Peter's house. Your handkerchief with traces of poison. Your convenient memory lapses about where you were and what you were doing. It doesn't paint a pretty picture."

I leaned forward, desperation creeping into my voice. "Sheriff, please. Think about it logically. If I were the killer, why would I dispose of evidence in my own trash can? Why wouldn't I have gotten rid of it somewhere else?"

Miller's eyes narrowed. "Maybe you panicked. Maybe you thought no one would look there. Or maybe you're just not as clever as you think you are."

The accusation stung. I was about to protest further when a sharp knock at the door interrupted us. Miller frowned, clearly annoyed at the interruption. "Come in," he called out.

A young officer poked his head into the room, looking slightly flustered. "Sorry to interrupt, Sheriff, but there are two people here who say they have an alibi for Mr. Butterfield. Say it's urgent."

Miller's frown deepened. "What people? What information?"

Before the officer could respond, a familiar voice piped up from the hallway. "That would be us, Sheriff. Emma Estrella, town astrologer and purveyor of cosmic wisdom, and Shawn O' Connell, proprietor of the Salty Breeze."

I couldn't believe my ears. Emma and Shawn? What on earth were they doing here?

Miller sighed, pinching the bridge of his nose. "Fine, let them in. But make it quick."

Emma swept into the room in a swirl of colorful scarves and jangling jewelry, followed by a somewhat bemused-looking Shawn. Emma's wild silver hair seemed to crackle with electricity, and her eyes, magnified behind thick glasses, darted around the room before settling on me.

"Jim, my dear!" she exclaimed. "I felt a disturbance in your aura and knew you were in trouble. The stars guided me here to set things right."

I blinked, momentarily stunned into silence. Miller looked like he was developing a headache.

"Ms. Estrella, Mr. O'Connell," he said, his voice strained, "you said you had an alibi for Mr. Butterfield?"

"Oh yes," Emma nodded vigorously. "It's about that handkerchief you found."

Sheriff Miller's brow furrowed. "How did you know we found a handkerchief, Ms. Estrella?"

Emma's eyes twinkled mischievously. "Oh, you know how it is in a small town, Sheriff. News travels faster than light itself. I overheard some chatter at the market this afternoon."

Sheriff Miller sighed, his expression a mix of resignation and skepticism. He gestured for Emma to continue, his patience visibly wearing thin.

"You see, Sheriff," Emma went on, undeterred, "I made this handkerchief for Jim as a welcoming present when he moved to town. I gave it to him at the Salty Breeze, just the day after Peter's death. Shawn here was witness to the whole thing."

I stared at Emma, my mind racing. This was a lie, of course – Martha had made that handkerchief years ago. But it was also a potential lifeline. I decided to play along.

"That's right," I said, nodding. "I can't believe I forgot about that. I'm sorry, Sheriff, my memory isn't what it used to be."

Miller's eyes narrowed suspiciously. "And why didn't you mention this before, Mr. Butterfield?"

I shrugged, trying to look appropriately sheepish. "As I said, my memory isn't the best these days. And with all the stress of being questioned about a murder, well... it must have slipped my mind."

Miller turned to Shawn, his expression skeptical. "Mr. O'Connell, is this true? Did you witness Ms. Estrella giving Mr. Butterfield this handkerchief?"

Shawn nodded, his usual easy-going manner replaced by a solemn seriousness. "That's right, Sheriff. It was just the day after Peter's death. Emma burst into the bar, all out of breath, saying she'd been looking for Jim all over town. Said she had a welcome gift for him and was relieved to finally track him down here. She gave him the handkerchief right there at the counter."

He paused, a hint of amusement crossing his face. "I remember it clearly because Emma insisted on doing some kind of blessing over it first. Said it would bring Jim good fortune in his new home." Shawn's expression sobered. "Given recent events, I suppose that blessing didn't quite pan out as intended."

Miller frowned, clearly conflicted. "This still doesn't explain how the handkerchief ended up in Mr. Butterfield's trash, covered in poison."

"But Sheriff," I added, seizing the opportunity, "don't you see? If Emma gave me that handkerchief just the day after Peter's death, I couldn't possibly have used it to kill Peter. The timing doesn't work."

Miller's frown deepened as he opened his mouth to speak. Before he could utter a word, there was a knock at the door. A young officer peeked his head in, his face etched with concern. "Excuse me, Sheriff. Could I have a word with you outside? It's urgent."

Miller nodded curtly and stood up. "Excuse me for a moment," he said, following the officer out of the room.

As Miller and the officer stepped out, I exchanged glances with Emma and Shawn. Emma gave me a reassuring wink, while Shawn offered a small nod of encouragement.

After what felt like an eternity, Miller returned, his expression stern. "Mr. Butterfield," he began, his voice tight, "while this new information doesn't clear you entirely, it does introduce some doubt into our timeline. More importantly, our lab results just came back, and the traces of poison on the handkerchief are inconsistent with the type of rat poison that killed Mr. Johnson."

Then why had they brought me in for questioning if they didn't have all their facts straight? Were they just so eager to close the case quickly that they'd jumped at the first piece of evidence that seemed to point to a culprit?

Sheriff paused, clearly frustrated. "Given this development, and the fact that we don't have enough solid evidence to hold you at this time, I'm going to have to release you."

A wave of relief washed over me, but Miller held up a hand, silencing me before I could say anything. "Don't get too comfortable, Mr. Butterfield. You're still a person of interest in this investigation. You're not to leave town under any circumstances. You'll make yourself available for questioning whenever we require it. And if we uncover any evidence that contradicts Ms. Estrella and Mr. O'Connell's story, you'll be right back in this room. Do I make myself clear?"

I nodded solemnly. "Crystal clear, Sheriff. Thank you."

As Emma, Shawn, and I made our way out of the police station, I couldn't shake the feeling that I'd just narrowly escaped disaster. But I also knew that this was far from over. Someone in Oceanview Cove was a killer, and they were trying to pin their crime on me.

As we stepped out into the cool night air, I turned to Emma and Shawn, a mix of gratitude and confusion swirling in my mind. "I can't thank you both enough for what you did in there. But... why? How did you know I needed help?"

Emma's eyes twinkled mysteriously behind her thick lenses. "The stars, my dear Jim. They whispered of your plight, and I knew I had to intervene."

I raised an eyebrow, skeptical despite my gratitude. "The stars told you I was in trouble?"

Emma chuckled, her numerous bangles jingling as she waved her hand dismissively. "Well, that and the fact that I happened to be taking an evening stroll to observe the celestial bodies when I saw the police car pull up to your house. I overheard the whole conversation about the handkerchief."

My eyes widened in surprise. "You were there? Why didn't you come forward right away?"

Emma's expression turned sheepish. "I'll admit, my first instinct was to hurry home and pretend I hadn't seen anything. It's not wise to meddle in police affairs, you know." She paused, her gaze drifting to a spot just beyond my shoulder. "But then, the most curious thing happened."

"What was that?" I asked, intrigued despite myself.

"Your cat appeared," Emma said, her voice filled with wonder. "He emerged from the shadows and began meowing at me most insistently. I felt a sudden wave of compassion, thinking of how he would be left alone if you were arrested. And then..." she trailed off, her eyes growing distant.

"Then what?" I prompted.

Emma's focus snapped back to me. "Then I had the strangest sensation that he was trying to communicate with me. That he wanted me to help you. Coupled with my earlier premonition of trouble heading your way, well, I knew I had to act."

I stared at her, torn between disbelief and a grudging sense of appreciation for her imagination. Before I could respond, I heard a familiar meow from behind me. I turned to see Ginger walking out of the shadows, his tail held high.

Emma gasped, her hand flying to her chest. "Great stars above! It's him – your cat! See how he comes when we speak of him? Truly, there's something special about this feline."

I watched as Ginger approached, looking rather pleased with himself. To me, he said, "Well, well. Maybe she's not such a fraud after all, this stargazer of yours." But to Emma and Shawn, it was just another meow.

Shawn, who had been quiet until now, spoke up. "As for me, well, I couldn't let a friend take the fall for something he didn't do. When Emma came to the bar and told me what was happening, I knew I had to help. Besides," he added with a wink, "what kind of bartender would I be if I couldn't provide an alibi when needed?"

I felt a lump form in my throat, touched by their kindness. "I don't know what to say. Thank you both, truly."

Shawn placed a reassuring hand on my shoulder. "We've got your back, Jim. Just... maybe stay away from the bar for a few days, yeah? Don't want to give the Sheriff any reason to doubt our story."

He glanced at an antique pocket watch he pulled from his vest. "Speaking of the bar, I should get going. Patrons are waiting, and these drinks won't serve themselves."

Emma nodded, her colorful scarves swaying with the movement. "I should be off too. Need to continue my stroll and observe the celestial bodies. The stars wait for no one, you know."

"I understand. Thank you both again. I don't know how I'll ever repay you." I said, grateful for their support.

Emma waved her hand dismissively. "Nonsense, dear. I'm just following the cosmic path laid out for me."

As Emma and Shawn headed off down the moonlit street, Emma with a final wave and a reminder to "keep an eye on the stars," and Shawn with a friendly nod, I couldn't help but feel a mix of gratitude and trepidation. We'd dodged one bullet tonight, but I had a feeling our troubles were far from over.

"Come on, Ginger," I said, stifling a yawn. "Let's go home."

As we turned to leave, something caught my eye. Near the corner of the police station, I noticed a shape that seemed out of place. It moved slightly, almost blending into the night. I squinted, trying to make out details, but in the split second it disappeared.

"Did you see that?" I whispered to Ginger, my heart suddenly racing.

Ginger's fur bristled. "I did. Want to check it out?"

I hesitated, then nodded. "We'd better. It could be important."

We made our way towards the spot where I'd seen the movement. As we rounded the corner of the police station, we found ourselves in a narrow, dimly lit alleyway.

"Look," Ginger said, nodding towards something on the ground.

I squinted in the poor light, then felt my blood run cold. There, lying on the dirty pavement, was a knife. But not just any knife – I recognized the worn handle and the glint of the steel blade. It was the same knife I'd seen on Robert Reeves' table at the docks.

With shaking hands, I knelt down to get a closer look. In the dim light, I could just make out two letters engraved on the handle: RR.

"Robert Reeves," I breathed, my mind reeling.

"This can't be a coincidence," Ginger said, his tail swishing agitatedly. "But what does it mean? Was Robert here? And if so, why?"

I shook my head, bewildered. "I don't know. But we can't leave it here."

"Agreed," Ginger said. "But we can't take it to the police either. You've only just gotten out of their crosshairs."

I nodded grimly. "You're right. We'll take it with us."

Carefully, I picked up the knife, wrapping it in a napkin before slipping it into my pocket. The weight of it felt like a lead weight, a tangible reminder of the danger we were in.

"What a night," I muttered as we started to make our way home.

Ginger rubbed against my leg sympathetically. "You can say that again. But look on the bright side – at least you're not spending it in a cell."

I managed a weak chuckle. "True enough. But now what? Do we go to the docks and confront Robert?"

"Hold your horses, old man," Ginger said. "First, we both need some rest. Confronting a potential murderer when you're stumbling around like a sleep-deprived penguin is a recipe for disaster."

As much as I wanted to argue, to push forward and solve this mystery once and all, I knew Ginger was right. My limbs felt like lead, and my mind was foggy with fatigue and stress. As we walked, the streets of Oceanview Cove seemed different somehow – darker, full of hidden dangers. The memory of that shadowy figure echoed in my mind, mingling with the weight of Robert's knife in my pocket.

As we reached the house, I fumbled with my keys, my hands still shaking slightly from the night's events. Once inside, I locked the door securely behind us, feeling a strange mix of relief and apprehension.

"Get some sleep, old man," Ginger said, jumping up onto the windowsill. "Tomorrow's going to be a big day."

Chapter 13

I awoke to the cheerful morning sun streaming through my bedroom window, its warm rays a stark contrast to the weight of last night's events. The old house creaked as I walked out of the bedroom, its familiar sounds a small comfort in the face of our ongoing mystery. As I shuffled into the kitchen, the worn floorboards cool beneath my feet, the quiet stillness of the morning seemed to amplify the gravity of our situation.

The kitchen, with its faded yellow wallpaper and well-loved appliances, felt like a snapshot from another era. It was easy to imagine Martha here, humming as she prepared breakfast, the room filled with the scent of bacon and the promise of a new day. Now, it felt eerily quiet, save for the gentle ticking of the old clock on the wall and the distant cry of seagulls.

Ginger was already perched on the kitchen counter, his orange fur catching the morning light, tail twitching with impatience. A half-eaten croissant dangled from his mouth. "About time you got up, old man," he mumbled around his pastry. "We've got a fisherman to interrogate, remember?"

I blinked, momentarily stunned by the sight. "I see you've helped yourself to breakfast. Those were meant for both of us, you know."

Ginger swallowed his mouthful, looking entirely unapologetic. "Early bird gets the worm. Or in this case, the early cat gets the croissant."

I grunted in response, pouring myself a cup of coffee. The mug, chipped and faded, had been a gift from Sarah years ago. 'World's Best Dad,' it proclaimed in now-faded letters. "Yes, yes. Let me wake up properly first. Not all of us can start the day with a stretch and a yawn."

As I sipped my coffee, leaning against the worn kitchen counter, I watched Ginger lick crumbs from his whiskers with an air of satisfaction. "You know," I mused, "for someone so keen on solving this mystery, you seem awfully content to stuff your face while I do all the heavy thinking."

Ginger's whiskers twitched in amusement. "What can I say? A detective needs fuel. Now, about our plan to confront Robert Reeves at the docks..."

I nodded, my mind shifting gears. The weight of Robert's knife, still wrapped in a napkin and hidden in my desk drawer, seemed to grow heavier with each passing moment.

"You know," I said, "I'm not sure this is such a good idea. Confronting a potential murderer? Maybe we should just turn the knife over to Sheriff Miller after all."

Ginger's green eyes narrowed. "And risk getting yourself thrown back in the interrogation room? No thanks. Besides, Miller's about as sharp as a rubber ball. We're better off handling this ourselves."

I sighed, knowing Ginger was right. Miller had been all too eager to pin Peter's murder on me. Who knows what he'd do with this new piece of evidence?

Just as I was about to respond, the sudden wail of sirens cut through the morning quiet. Ginger and I exchanged alarmed glances before rushing to the front window. A parade of police cars and an ambulance sped past, their lights flashing urgently against the pastel-colored houses of Oceanview Cove.

"What in the world?" I muttered, watching as they screeched to a halt further down the street.

Ginger's fur bristled, as he watched out of the window. "They're stopping at Ryan's house."

A chill ran down my spine. Without a word, I slipped on my shoes and headed for the door, Ginger hot on my heels.

As we approached Ryan's house, a crowd of neighbors had already gathered, their faces a mix of curiosity and concern. Yellow police tape stretched across Ryan's front yard, fluttering in the sea breeze. The sweet scent of blooming roses from nearby gardens mingled uneasily with the harsh reality of the police presence.

I spotted Sheriff Miller standing near his cruiser, his face grim as he spoke into his radio. His uniform, usually crisp and neat, looked rumpled, as if he'd been called out of bed in a hurry. Gathering my courage, I approached him, Ginger slinking along beside me.

"Sheriff? What's happening?"

Miller's eyes narrowed as he saw me, his mouth tightening into a thin line. "Mr. Butterfield. I thought I told you to stay out of police business."

"I live just down the street," I protested, gesturing towards my house. "I saw the commotion and wanted to make sure everything was alright."

Miller sighed, running a hand over his face. He suddenly looked older, more tired, the lines around his eyes deeper than I remembered. "It's Ryan Perkins. He's dead."

The words hit me like a physical blow. "Dead? But how?"

"Apparent suicide," Miller said, his voice flat. "Hanging. We found a note."

My mind reeled. Just last night, I'd seen Ryan peeking out from behind his curtains as the Sheriff drove me away, no doubt already planning how to spin that latest development for his newspaper. But now he was dead? It didn't seem possible.

"A note?" I repeated, struggling to process the information. "What did it say?"

Miller hesitated, clearly debating how much to reveal. "Look, Butterfield, I know we've been hard on you and I probably shouldn't be telling you this. But given our conversation yesterday and the fact that you were our primary suspect, it's only fair you're informed." He paused, his expression grim. "It was a confession. To Peter's murder."

I felt as if the ground had dropped out from under me. "What? That's impossible. Ryan didn't kill Peter."

Miller's eyes met mine, a mix of professional detachment and what might have been a hint of regret. "The note explicitly states that Ryan, and Ryan alone, was responsible for Peter's death. Said he couldn't live with the guilt anymore."

"Oh, please," Ginger muttered, his tail swishing irritably. "Ryan couldn't kill a spider without writing a three-page exposé about it first."

I stifled a smile at Ginger's comment, focusing on Miller. "Can I see the note?"

Miller shook his head, his jowls quivering slightly with the movement. "Absolutely not. This is our main evidence."

"But you've already decided it's a suicide, right?" I pressed. "So what's the harm?"

Miller's jaw clenched, a vein pulsing in his temple. "The case is closed, Mr. Butterfield. Ryan confessed. It's over."

A detail nagged at me. "Sheriff, the note... was it handwritten?"

Miller's expression flickered for a moment, like a fish darting beneath the surface of a pond. "No, it was typed and printed. Why?"

I filed this information away, my suspicions growing. "Just curious. It's just... Ryan always wrote everything by hand. I never saw him use a computer for his notes."

"People change their habits," Miller said dismissively, waving a hand as if to brush away my concerns. "Now, if you'll excuse me, I have work to do."

As Miller turned away, a realization struck me. "Wait, Sheriff. Does this mean I'm no longer a suspect in Peter's murder?"

Miller had the grace to look slightly abashed, his cheeks reddening. "Yes, well... consider yourself cleared. But don't think this gives you license to play detective, you hear?"

With that, he strode off, barking orders at young officers.

I stood there for a moment, staring at Ryan's house. The cheerful yellow paint now seemed garish, a mockery of the tragedy within. The rose bushes in the front yard, usually so meticulously pruned, looked wild and unkempt, as if they too were in mourning.

With a heavy sigh, I turned away from the scene and began the short walk home, Ginger walking silently beside me. The weight of the morning's revelations seemed to slow my steps, and by the time we reached our front porch, my mind was buzzing with questions. Ryan's death couldn't be a coincidence. But if he hadn't killed Peter, who had? And why frame Ryan?

The morning sun, once so cheerful, now cast long shadows across the room, as if the very light was trying to hide from the darkness that had descended upon Oceanview Cove. As I settled into my armchair, Ginger leapt onto the coffee table, his green eyes fixed intently on me.

"A typed suicide note?" Ginger scoffed, his whiskers twitching in disbelief. "Ryan was so old school, he probably thought 'typing' meant using one of those ancient typewriters with the clicky keys. I hadn't noticed any computers in his house or his office. His assistants at the Gazette were probably doing all the typing, while he sent them handwritten notes with instructions."

"My thoughts exactly," I murmured, running a hand through my thinning hair. "Ryan wrote everything by hand. And a confession to Peter's murder? And then killing himself? It's too neat, too convenient."

"So what now?" Ginger asked, his green eyes glinting with determination. "Still fancy a chat with our friendly neighborhood fisherman?"

I straightened up, casting one last glance at Ryan's house. The ambulance was pulling away, its lights no longer flashing, carrying a silent burden. "More than ever. Something's not right here, Ginger. And I have a feeling Robert Reeves might have some answers."

"And if he doesn't?" Ginger asked, his tail twitching.

"Then we keep digging," I said, a determination I didn't entirely feel creeping into my voice. "Someone in this town knows the truth, and we're going to find out who."

Ginger yawned, stretching lazily. "Well, at least you're not boring in your old age. Most retirees take up golf or bird watching. You? You're solving murders and antagonizing the local law enforcement."

Despite the gravity of the situation, I couldn't help but chuckle. "What can I say? After years of living vicariously through mystery novels, I suppose I've decided to write my own story. Though I must admit, I preferred it when the danger was safely confined to the pages of a book."

I made my way to the bedroom and opened the desk drawer. I carefully retrieved Robert's knife, still wrapped in its napkin and slipped it into a small bag.

As I prepared for our trip to the docks, a sobering thought struck me. "Ginger," I said, my voice low, "if Robert really is the killer, he's already taken out two of my neighbors. What if... what if I'm next?"

Ginger's green eyes met mine, a fierce protectiveness in their depths. "Not on my watch, old man. We're in this together, remember? Besides," he added, a hint of his usual snark returning, "I still haven't gotten you to splurge on the fancy cat food. You're not allowed to die until I've tasted the good stuff."

I smiled, grateful for Ginger's unique brand of comfort. "Well, we can't have that, can we? Alright, let's go beard the lion in his den."

As we headed out the door, the weight of Robert's knife in my bag seemed to grow heavier. I couldn't shake the feeling that we were walking into danger. But what choice did we have? With Ryan gone and Sheriff Miller all too eager to close the case, it was up to us to uncover the truth.

Chapter 14

The familiar quaint streets of Oceanview Cove seemed sinister as Ginger and I made our way towards the docks. Every shadow seemed to hide a potential threat, every passerby a possible accomplice. I found myself jumping at the slightest sound, my nerves frayed to the breaking point.

"Relax, will you?" Ginger hissed as I nearly leapt out of my skin at the sound of a car backfiring. "You look about as inconspicuous as a zebra at a horse convention."

I took a deep breath, trying to calm my racing heart. The salty sea air filled my nostrils, mingling with the ever-present scent of fish. Seagulls cried overhead, their mournful calls adding to the eerie atmosphere.

As we neared the docks, something felt off. The usual bustle of activity was noticeably absent. Where there should have been fishermen preparing their boats, mending nets, and loading supplies, there was only an unsettling quiet.

"Where is everyone?" I muttered, more to myself than to Ginger.

The cat's ears twitched as he surveyed the scene. "Good question. This place is usually busier than a flea market on discount day."

We made our way down the wooden planks, the boards creaking ominously under our feet. The boats bobbed gently in the water, their ropes straining with each small wave. But Robert's familiar fishing boat was conspicuously absent from its usual spot.

A knot formed in my stomach. "Ginger, you don't think..."

Before I could finish my thought, a gruff voice called out from behind us. "You lookin' for someone?"

I turned to see an older fisherman, his face weathered by years at sea, watching us with a mix of curiosity and suspicion.

"Yes, actually," I said, trying to keep my voice steady. "I'm looking for Robert Reeves. Have you seen him?"

The man's bushy eyebrows furrowed. "Robert? He took off early this morning. 'Round 4 AM, I reckon. Said he was headed out to the deeper waters with his boy."

My heart sank. Robert had left in the middle of the night? With his son? The implications were troubling, to say the least.

"That's... unusual, isn't it?" I probed, trying to keep my tone casual.

The fisherman shrugged. "Not for Robert. He likes to get an early start when he's taking his boy out. Says the fish bite better at dawn."

I exchanged a glance with Ginger, whose tail was twitching with barely contained agitation. Could Robert have killed Ryan last night, planted the suicide note, and then fled with his son under the guise of an early fishing trip?

"Any idea when he'll be back?" I asked, trying to keep the desperation out of my voice.

"Oh, he won't be long," the fisherman assured me. "When Robert takes off that early, he's usually back before most of us even get started. I'd give him another ten minutes or so."

I nodded, thanking the man for his help. As he walked away, I turned to Ginger, my mind racing.

"What do you think?" I whispered.

Ginger's green eyes narrowed. "I think we wait. If Robert doesn't show up soon, we might have to consider taking this to the police after all."

We found a spot to wait, perching on some crates near the edge of the dock. The minutes ticked by agonizingly slowly, each passing moment adding to my anxiety. What if Robert didn't come back? What if he had really fled?

Just as I was about to suggest we give up and head to the police station, a familiar boat appeared on the horizon. Relief flooded through me, quickly followed by a new wave of apprehension. This was it. We were about to confront our prime suspect.

As Robert's boat drew closer, I could make out two figures on board. Robert's imposing form was unmistakable, but beside him was a much smaller figure – a boy of about eight or nine, his face bright with excitement.

The boat docked smoothly, and Robert helped his son off before tying up. The boy was chattering animatedly, clearly thrilled with their early morning adventure.

"And did you see that big one, Dad? It was huge!" the boy exclaimed, his hands spread wide to indicate the size of their catch.

Robert's face, usually set in a scowl, softened as he looked at his son. "Sure did, champ. You did a great job reeling that one in."

The transformation was startling. This gentle, proud father was a far cry from the gruff, intimidating man I'd encountered before. It made me question everything I thought I knew about Robert Reeves.

Taking a deep breath, I approached them. "Robert? Can I have a word?"

Robert's head snapped up, his expression immediately hardening as he saw me. "You again? What do you want now?"

I glanced at the boy, who was looking between us with curiosity. "It's about... that thing we discussed before. I found something that belongs to you."

Understanding dawned in Robert's eyes. He turned to his son. "Hey, buddy, why don't you go show Mr. Davis our catch? I bet he'd love to see it."

The boy nodded eagerly and scampered off, leaving Robert and me alone. Well, alone except for Ginger, who was watching the proceedings with keen interest.

"Alright," Robert said, his voice low. "What's this about?"

I reached into my bag and pulled out the wrapped knife. Robert's eyes widened as I unwrapped it.

"Where did you get that?" he demanded.

"I found it near the police station around midnight," I said, watching his reaction carefully. "Right after I was released from questioning about Peter's murder. I saw a dark figure that might have dropped it. Was that you, Robert?"

Robert's brow furrowed, a mix of confusion and indignation crossing his face. "Me? No, it couldn't have been. I went to bed early last night. Had to wake up at the crack of dawn to go fishing with my son. You can ask him yourself if you don't believe me."

His reaction seemed genuine. There was no hint of the guilt or panic I'd expected to see. After a moment's hesitation, I held out the knife to Robert. My fingers lingered on the handle for a second before I let go, a part of me still wary of handing a potential weapon to a possible suspect.

Robert took the knife, turning it over in his hands. "This is mine. I left it in my boat yesterday evening and couldn't find it this morning. Thought I'd just misplaced it."

Ginger, sitting at my feet, muttered under his breath, "He's telling the truth, old man. Unless he's a better actor than half of Hollywood."

I nodded slightly, acknowledging Ginger's assessment while keeping my eyes on Robert.

"Robert," I said, deciding to push further, "I need to ask you about something. There's been talk about property dealings down at the docks. Something Peter was involved in. Did you two argue about that?"

Robert's face screwed up in confusion. "Property dealings? At the docks? I've never heard anything about that. Who told you that?"

I hesitated, realizing too late that I might be revealing too much. "Ryan mentioned it."

"Ryan?" Robert's eyebrows shot up. "The newspaper guy? Well, he must have gotten his wires crossed, because there's nothing like that happening here."

I nodded. Why would Ryan have lied about the property dealings? Could he have been the one to drop the knife by the police station? But if so, why? And why kill himself afterward? None of it made sense. As these questions swirled in my head, I realized there was one crucial piece of information Robert didn't know—assuming he truly wasn't the killer.

I leaned in closer, lowering my voice. "Robert, there's something you should know. Ryan... he was found dead this morning. They're saying it was suicide."

Robert's eyes widened in genuine shock, his face paling visibly. "What? Ryan's dead? But... how? I just saw him yesterday at the market. He seemed fine, his usual nosy self."

His reaction confirmed what I had suspected – Robert couldn't have known about Ryan's death, having been out at sea all morning. The surprise in his voice was unmistakable, and I found myself believing him despite my earlier suspicions.

"I'm sorry to be the bearer of bad news," I said softly. "But let's get back to Peter for a moment. If you and Peter didn't argue about property dealings," I pressed, "what did you argue about?"

Robert sighed, running a hand through his salt-and-pepper hair. "It was stupid, really. My boy and his friends like to play near Peter's house. They can get a bit rowdy sometimes, and it was disrupting Peter's afternoon nap. I told him they're just kids, to let them play. That's all it was."

I blinked, taken aback. After all the theories and suspicions, could it really have been something so mundane?

"That's... it?" I asked, unable to keep the disbelief out of my voice.

Robert nodded. "That's it. Look, I know I can come off as a bit of a grump, but I'm not some kind of murderer. Peter and I had our differences, but I'd never hurt him."

As if to underscore his point, Robert's son came bounding back at that moment, full of excitement about showing off their catch. The tenderness with which Robert interacted with his boy was undeniable. It was hard to reconcile this image with that of a cold-blooded killer.

Robert turned back to me, his expression softening. "Listen, I appreciate you bringing my knife back. It was a gift from my late father after my first big catch. Means a lot to me."

I nodded, feeling a twinge of guilt for having suspected him. "I'm glad I could return it to you. Family heirlooms like that are irreplaceable."

There was a moment of awkward silence as we both realized our conversation had reached its natural end. I glanced at Ginger, who was eyeing a nearby seagull with predatory interest, and decided it was time to wrap things up.

"Well," I said, feeling suddenly deflated, "thank you for your time, Robert. And for clearing things up."

As Ginger and I made our way back up the dock, my mind was whirling. We'd come here looking for answers, but instead, we'd only found more questions. Why had Ryan lied about the property dealings? Was it just a misunderstanding, or was there something more sinister at play?

The walk back home was quiet, both Ginger and I lost in our thoughts. As we approached my house, Ginger finally broke the silence. "Well, old man, it looks like we've hit another dead end."

I nodded, feeling the weight of our failed investigation settling on my shoulders. "I don't understand it, Ginger.

Every time we think we're getting close to the truth, it slips away from us."

"Maybe we're looking at this all wrong," Ginger mused as we climbed the porch steps. "Maybe the answer isn't in what we're seeing, but in what we're not seeing."

I paused, my hand on the doorknob, considering Ginger's words. He had a point. We'd been so focused on finding the killer that we might have overlooked other important details.

As we stepped inside, the familiar surroundings of my home offered little comfort. The mystery of Peter's death, and now Ryan's, loomed larger than ever. I sank into my well-worn armchair, the leather creaking in protest.

Ginger leapt onto the coffee table, his tail swishing back and forth as he fixed me with his piercing green gaze. "Alright, old man, let's review what we know."

I sighed, running a hand through my thinning hair. "What we know? It feels like we know less now than when we started, Ginger."

The cat's whiskers twitched in annoyance. "Don't be dramatic. We've learned plenty. We know Robert's knife was dropped near the police station, but Robert seems genuinely innocent. We know Ryan lied about the property dealings at the docks. And we know someone wanted Ryan silenced badly enough to stage his suicide."

I nodded slowly, trying to piece it all together in my mind. The midday sun streamed through the windows, bathing the room in a warm, golden glow. Outside, I could hear the distant cry of seagulls and the gentle lapping of waves against the shore. It all seemed so peaceful, so at odds with the turmoil in my mind.

"But why?" I mused aloud. "Why would Ryan lie about the property dealings? And if he wasn't the killer, who is? And why frame him?"

Ginger stretched lazily, his claws extending before retracting. "Those, my dear Watson, are the questions we need to answer."

I couldn't help but chuckle at that. "Watson, am I? I thought I was supposed to be the detective in this partnership."

"Keep dreaming, old man," Ginger retorted, but there was a glimmer of amusement in his eyes.

The levity was short-lived, however, as the weight of our investigation settled back over me like a heavy blanket. I felt the weariness deep in my bones, a fatigue that went beyond the physical.

"Maybe we're in over our heads, Ginger," I said softly, voicing the doubt that had been gnawing at me. "We're not real detectives. I'm just a retired librarian, and you're... well, a cat. Perhaps we should leave this to the professionals."

Ginger's tail stopped twitching, his eyes narrowing. "The professionals? You mean like Sheriff Miller, who was ready to throw you in jail on flimsy evidence? The same Sheriff who's content to write off two suspicious deaths as open-and-shut cases?"

I winced at the cat's harsh tone. "When you put it that way…"

"Besides," Ginger continued, his voice softening slightly, "we've come too far to stop now. Think about it, Jim. Peter and Ryan are dead. Someone in this town is responsible, and they're walking free while an innocent man's name is being dragged through the mud. Can you really walk away from that?"

I leaned back in my chair, letting my gaze drift to the window. The view of the sea, usually so calming, now seemed to mock me with its serenity. How could the world look so peaceful when such darkness lurked beneath the surface?

"No," I admitted finally. "No, I can't walk away. But Ginger, I feel so… powerless. Every lead we follow seems to lead to a dead end. It's like trying to solve a jigsaw puzzle with half the pieces missing."

Ginger hopped down from the coffee table and walked over to me, surprising me by jumping into my lap. It was a rare display of affection from the usually snarky cat.

"That's why you've got me," he said, settling himself comfortably. "With your human intuition and my feline instincts, we'll crack this case."

I smiled, touched by Ginger's unwavering faith in our unlikely partnership. Still, the events of the day had taken their toll. My mind felt like a tangled ball of yarn, with threads of information knotted together in a confusing mess.

"Perhaps you're right," I said, stifling a yawn. "But right now, I think what I need most is a nap. Maybe a fresh perspective will help us see what we've been missing."

Ginger nodded, jumping down from my lap. "Not a bad idea. I could use a catnap myself. Just don't sleep too long. We've got a mystery to solve."

As I made my way to the bedroom, the weariness of the past few days seemed to settle into my very bones. Lying down, I couldn't help but wonder what Martha would think of all this. Would she be proud of my efforts to uncover the truth? Or would she scold me for getting mixed up in such a dangerous situation?

Chapter 15

I found myself standing on the shore of Oceanview Cove, the cool sand beneath my feet and the salty breeze tousling my hair. The sky was a watercolor masterpiece of pinks and oranges, the setting sun casting a golden glow across the gentle waves. It was beautiful, peaceful, and entirely surreal.

"Jim."

The soft, familiar voice sent a jolt through my heart. I turned slowly, hardly daring to believe it. And there she was – Martha, my Martha, standing a few yards away. She looked just as she had in her prime, her silver hair catching the light of the setting sun, her eyes twinkling with that mischievous spark I'd fallen in love with all those years ago.

"Martha?" I whispered, my voice catching in my throat.

She smiled, that warm, loving smile that had always been my anchor. "Hello, my love. Enjoying your retirement?"

Before I could respond, she turned and began walking along the shoreline, her bare feet leaving delicate imprints in the wet sand.

"Martha, wait!" I called out, hurrying after her. "I don't understand. What's happening?"

She glanced back at me, her expression both amused and slightly exasperated – a look I knew all too well. "You're dreaming, Jimmy. But that doesn't mean this isn't important. Come on, keep up. We have a lot to discuss and not much time."

As I fell into step beside her, she spoke again. "You've stirred up quite the hornet's nest, haven't you? Two deaths, a town full of secrets, and you right in the middle of it all."

"I didn't mean to," I protested weakly. "I just wanted to help."

Martha chuckled. "Of course you did. That's who you are, Jim. Always trying to set things right. It's one of the things I love about you."

We walked in silence for a moment, the rhythmic sound of the waves a soothing backdrop to our surreal reunion.

"I miss you," I said softly. "Every day."

Martha's hand found mine, her touch as warm and comforting as I remembered. "I know, love. I miss you too. But you're not done yet. There's still work to be done."

"The mystery," I said. "Peter and Ryan's deaths. But I'm at a dead end, Martha. Every lead turns into nothing. I don't know where to go from here."

She stopped walking and turned to face me, her eyes searching mine. "Don't you? Think, Jim. What haven't you explored yet? Where haven't you looked?"

I frowned, trying to piece together her cryptic words. "We've talked to almost everyone in town. We've been to the docks, the bar, even broken into Ryan's house. And Ginger's managed to sneak into Peter's place..."

"What about Peter's computer?" Martha interjected. "Remember what Ginger said about Peter always hiding his computer activity?"

The realization hit me like a wave. "Peter's computer? But it's probably been taken by the police. At least, that's always what happens in my mystery novels."

Martha's eyes twinkled. "Perhaps. But there might be other devices, hidden away. You need to go back to Peter's house, Jim. The answers you're looking for, the key to this whole mystery – it's in his digital world."

As the meaning of her words sank in, I noticed that Martha had slowed her pace, allowing me to draw closer. The sun was sinking lower on the horizon, painting the sky in deeper shades of red and purple.

"But what am I looking for?" I asked. "What's this key you mentioned?"

Martha smiled enigmatically. "You'll know it when you see it. Trust your instincts, Jimmy. They've gotten you this far."

We walked a bit further, the sound of the waves growing louder in my ears. "I'm afraid, Martha," I admitted. "What if I'm wrong? What if I can't solve this?"

She stopped and turned to me, her eyes filled with warmth and confidence. "You can, and you will. You're stronger than you think, Jim. And you're not alone. That cat of yours is quite the detective himself."

I chuckled. "Ginger would be pleased to hear you say that."

Martha's expression grew serious. "Listen to me, Jim. The truth is within your reach. But you need to be careful. Not everyone in Oceanview Cove is what they seem. Trust your instincts, and trust Ginger. You two make quite the team."

The sun was nearly gone now, the last rays of light stretching across the water. Martha's form seemed to shimmer in the fading light.

"You're leaving, aren't you?" I asked, a lump forming in my throat.

She nodded, her smile tinged with sadness. "It's time. But remember, I'm always with you, Jim. Always."

I stepped forward, pulling her into an embrace. She felt so real, so solid in my arms. I could smell the familiar scent of her perfume, feel the softness of her hair against my cheek. As I leaned in to kiss her, my eyes closed...

The world seemed to shift, and suddenly, I was aware of the soft pillow beneath my head, the warm rays filtering through the curtains.

I woke up.

The bedroom was bathed in the soft glow of late afternoon sunlight. For a moment, I lay still, the dream still vivid in my mind. I could almost feel the imprint of Martha's hand in mine, smell the salt of the sea air.

"About time you woke up," Ginger's voice came from somewhere near my feet. "I was beginning to think you'd slipped into a coma."

I sat up, rubbing the sleep from my eyes. "Ginger, I think I know what we need to do next."

The cat's ears perked up. "Oh? And what brilliant plan did you come up with while snoring loud enough to wake the dead?"

"We need to break into Peter's house again," I said, then quickly added, "We need to check Peter's computer."

Ginger's tail twitched. "Hate to break it to you, old man, but when I snuck in there before, the computer was gone. The police probably took it to the station for checking."

I nodded, a rueful smile crossing my face. "Just as I thought. In my mystery novels, the police always—"

But Ginger wasn't finished. "But," he continued, his whiskers twitching thoughtfully, "I do remember seeing Peter use a tablet quite often. He had a clever hiding spot for it – inside a hollowed-out book on his shelf. The police might not have found it."

My excitement returned in full force. "That's it! That must be what Martha was hinting at in my dream. We need to get that tablet, Ginger."

Ginger's eyes narrowed. "You do realize this would be our second break-in into Peter's house, right? And this time, you'll have to come with me. As talented as I am, I can't exactly use a touch screen with these paws."

I nodded, feeling a mix of nervousness and determination. "I know. But it's our best shot at finding out the truth."

Ginger seemed to consider this for a moment. "Alright, I'm in. But if we get caught, I'm blaming this whole escapade on your midlife crisis."

I chuckled, reaching out to scratch behind his ears. "Deal."

As I stood and stretched, I felt a renewed sense of purpose coursing through me. The weight of the investigation, which had seemed so heavy just hours ago, now felt more like a challenge to be met.

"You really think we'll find something on that tablet?" Ginger asked, a hint of skepticism still in his voice.

I nodded, thinking back to Martha's words. "I do. Whatever's going on in this town, whatever led to Peter and Ryan's deaths – I think the answers are in Peter's digital world. We just need to find them."

Ginger hopped down from the bed, stretching languidly. "Well, I suppose if we're going to commit more felonies, we might as well do it thoroughly. When do we leave?"

I glanced out the window. The sun was just beginning to set, painting the sky in shades of orange and pink reminiscent of my dream. "We'll wait until it's fully dark. Around midnight should do it."

Breaking into Peter's house was a risk, just like last time. If we were caught, we'd have a lot of explaining to do. But the potential reward – solving the mystery that had turned our lives upside down – was worth it.

I thought about Martha, about the confidence she'd shown in me in the dream. Whether it was really her spirit guiding me or just my subconscious working through the puzzle, I didn't know. But I was grateful for the push in the right direction.

"You know," Ginger said as he watched me gather supplies, "if Peter had told me a month ago that I'd be planning another burglary in his house with a retired librarian, I'd have said he was crazy."

I laughed, the sound echoing in the quiet house. "Life's full of surprises, isn't it? Who knows, maybe we'll start a new career as cat burglars."

Ginger groaned at the pun. "Let's solve one mystery before we start planning our life of crime, shall we?"

As the sun dipped below the horizon, I felt a sense of anticipation building. Whatever we found in Peter's house tonight, I knew it would change everything. The quiet retirement I'd envisioned when I moved here seemed like a distant memory now.

But as I looked at Ginger, my unlikely partner in this investigation, I realized I wouldn't have it any other way. After all, I thought with a wry smile, what else does a retired librarian have to do but solve murders and uncover town conspiracies?

Chapter 16

Darkness blanketed Oceanview Cove as Ginger and I crept towards Peter's house. Our street was eerily quiet, save for the distant crash of waves against the shore and the occasional hoot of an owl. The salty sea breeze carried a hint of early autumn chill, making me pull my jacket tighter around my shoulders.

"Remind me again why I'm breaking into a dead man's house at my age?" I whispered to Ginger, my heart pounding so loudly I was sure it would wake the entire neighborhood.

Ginger's tail swished in the darkness, his green eyes glowing with a mixture of amusement and determination. "Because you're having a midlife crisis at sixty-eight, old man. Now keep it down, will you? We're supposed to be stealthy."

I chuckled softly, despite the gravity of our situation. It was true. When I'd imagined my retirement, I'd pictured quiet evenings with a good book, maybe the occasional game of chess at the local park. Breaking and entering certainly hadn't been on the agenda.

As we approached Peter's house, I was surprised to see it unguarded. The yellow police tape fluttered in the breeze, reminding of the tragedy that had occurred here, but there wasn't an officer in sight. The windows were dark, the house looming before us like a sleeping giant.

"Looks like the Sheriff's boys are all busy over at Ryan's place," Ginger observed, his whiskers twitching. "Lucky for us."

I nodded, feeling a twinge of guilt at the thought of Ryan. His death still weighed heavily on my mind, another piece in this increasingly complex puzzle. But now wasn't the time for regrets or second-guessing. We had a mission to complete.

I watched in amazement as Ginger slipped through the pet flap in the front door with practiced ease. His orange fur seemed to glow for a moment in the moonlight before disappearing into the darkness of the house. A moment later, I heard the soft click of a window being unlocked.

"Your turn, Jim," Ginger's voice drifted from inside. "Try not to get stuck this time."

Taking a deep breath, I glanced around one last time to ensure we weren't being watched. The street remained deserted, the neighboring houses dark and silent. It was now or never.

I hoisted myself onto the windowsill, wincing slightly as my joints protested the unusual activity. To my surprise, I slid through with relative ease, landing quietly on the floor inside. The room smelled musty, with a lingering scent of

Peter's cologne – a poignant reminder of the man who once lived here.

"Would you look at that," I muttered, brushing myself off. "I guess all this stress has been good for something. I must have lost a few pounds."

Ginger snorted, his tail swishing in amusement. "Don't get too excited. You're still no cat burglar. Now, let's find that tablet before someone decides to do a late-night patrol."

We made our way through the darkened house, our footsteps muffled by the thick carpet. Family photos lined the walls, Peter's smiling face a stark contrast to the somber atmosphere that now permeated the home. I tried not to look too closely at them, focusing instead on our goal.

Finally, we reached Peter's study, and I couldn't help but gasp at the sight. The room was a mess, just as Ginger had described. Papers were strewn everywhere, books lay haphazardly on the floor, and the desk looked like it had been ransacked. The moonlight streaming through the window cast eerie shadows across the chaos, giving the room an almost surreal quality.

"It's like a tornado hit in here," I whispered, carefully stepping over a fallen stack of folders. "Are you sure the police didn't do this when they searched the place?"

Ginger shook his head, walking over to the bookshelf. His green eyes scanned the spines as he said, "No, it was like this when I first came in after Peter died. He must have been looking for something important before... well, you know."

The implication hung heavy in the air. Had Peter known he was in danger? Had he been searching for something that could have saved his life? Or perhaps, more chillingly, had the killer ransacked the room after Peter's death, desperately seeking something Peter had hidden?

"Here," Ginger said, interrupting my dark thoughts. He nodded towards a thick, leather-bound volume. "This is where he kept the tablet."

I reached for the book, my hands shaking slightly. As I pulled it from the shelf, I felt the weight shift oddly. It was heavier than a normal book, but with a strange imbalance. Opening it revealed a hollowed-out interior, and nestled inside was a sleek, modern tablet.

"Clever hiding spot," I murmured, lifting the device out. It felt cool and smooth in my hands, a piece of technology that seemed almost alien in this room full of paper and ink.

It was only then, holding the tablet in my hands, that I remembered my longstanding struggle with technology. I'd barely mastered working on a computer, and tablets were in a whole new league. I still used my ancient flip phone, for crying out loud. The device in my hands suddenly felt like a ticking time bomb, ready to explode with my incompetence.

"Uh, Ginger?" I said, my voice wavering. "I'm not sure I know how to use this thing."

Ginger sighed, a sound of pure feline exasperation. "For the love of catnip, Jim. It's not rocket science. Just turn it on and see what happens."

With trembling fingers, I searched the edges of the tablet for a button. Finding one that seemed promising, I pressed it, holding my breath. The screen flickered to life, illuminating the dark room with an eerie blue glow. My momentary triumph was short-lived, however, as a lock screen appeared, demanding a password.

"Great," I muttered, staring at the glowing screen. "Now what?"

"Try typing something," Ginger suggested, his tail swishing impatiently. "Use your fingers on the screen, like you're pressing invisible buttons."

I tapped at the screen, my clumsy fingers feeling like sausages compared to the delicate keyboard.

"Let me guess," Ginger said, his whiskers twitching thoughtfully. "Try... G-I-N-G-E-R."

I carefully typed in the letters, holding my breath as I hit enter. The screen flashed red. Two more tries.

"Okay, how about... O-R-A-N-G-E-C-A-T," Ginger suggested next.

Another flash of red. One attempt left. Panic began to set in. If we couldn't unlock this tablet, our entire mission would be for nothing.

"Ginger, you've got to get it right this time," I pleaded, feeling beads of sweat forming on my forehead. "You knew Peter better than anyone."

Ginger's eyes narrowed in concentration. "Alright, last try. G-I-N-G-E-R-C-A-T."

I raised an eyebrow at him, but carefully typed in the letters, holding my breath as I hit enter. The screen paused for a moment, the spinning wheel of doom making my heart race. Then suddenly, it came to life, revealing a colorful array of icons.

"You did it!" I exclaimed, resisting the urge to scoop Ginger up and hug him. "How did you know?"

"Just a hunch," Ginger said, but I could hear the relief in his voice. "Peter always said I was the most important thing in his life. Now, let's see what secrets he was hiding."

We looked at the array of icons on the screen, but I felt lost. "Ginger, how do I move through these?"

"Use your finger to swipe across the screen," Ginger instructed patiently. "Like you're brushing away crumbs."

I did as he said, marveling as the icons slid by. "This one says 'Gallery'," I pointed out. "Should we try that?"

At Ginger's nod, I tapped the icon. Suddenly the screen was filled with photos. Most were ordinary snapshots of life in Oceanview Cove – sunsets over the harbor, seagulls in flight, and plenty of pictures of Ginger lounging in various spots around the house. It was strange, seeing the world through Peter's eyes like this. These everyday moments, now frozen in time, took on a bittersweet significance.

But then something caught my eye. A thumbnail that looked different from the rest. I tapped on it, and the image expanded to fill the screen. "Ginger, this looks like some kind of document, but I can't read it. How do I make it bigger?"

"Use two fingers and spread them apart on the screen," Ginger explained. "It's called zoom in."

I followed his instructions, and the image zoomed in. As I read the now-legible text, I felt my heart skip a beat.

"Ginger," I whispered, my voice tight with excitement, "look at this. It's a contract for the sale of the house. And Maggie is listed as a co-owner!"

Ginger's tail swished excitedly, his eyes widening as he peered at the screen. "I knew it! I knew there was something fishy about that bakery witch." He turned and began rummaging through the papers scattered on the floor, his movements quick and purposeful. After a moment, he emerged with a document in his mouth. "I found it!" he said, his voice muffled. He dropped the paper on my lap. "This is the contract. I didn't find it last time because I'd already found that letter and the payment records. I thought that was enough. If only I'd dug a little deeper, we might have been closer to the truth sooner."

As I examined the physical contract, my finger accidentally brushed against another icon on the tablet's screen. Suddenly, a new window popped up – a messaging app, its interface cluttered with conversation threads.

"Oh," I said, startled by the sudden change. "I think I just opened Peter's messages."

Ginger was by my side in an instant. "What do you see?"

I scrolled through the conversations, my eyes widening as I took in the content. "There's a thread here with Maggie," I said, tapping to open it. As I read through the messages, a frown creased my brow. "This is odd. Peter's writing all these sweet things, calling her 'my darling' and 'sweetheart', but Maggie's responses are so... cold."

"That must be what Peter was always typing on his computer," Ginger mused, his tail swishing thoughtfully. "But wait a minute – if they were messaging like this, why would Peter write her an old-fashioned letter?"

I thought about it for a moment, remembering the half-written letter we'd discovered earlier. "Maybe he was trying to impress her? Given how detached she seems in these messages, perhaps he thought a handwritten letter would be more romantic."

As I continued to scroll through the messages, a familiar image caught my eye. "Look, Ginger. Peter sent Maggie that same photo of the contract we just saw. It says it was sent just three days before he died."

Maggie's response was a simple heart.

"A heart?" Ginger asked, peering at the screen. "That's it?"

I nodded, puzzled. "It's just a little picture of a heart. Is that significant?"

Ginger sighed. "It's called an emoji, Jim. It's a way of expressing emotions in text messages. A heart usually means affection or agreement."

I raised an eyebrow at Ginger. "How do you know all this stuff about technology?"

Ginger's tail twitched. "Peter taught me, believe it or not. Before he became all secretive and apparently obsessed with Maggie. He used to chat with me about all sorts of things while he was on his devices."

I nodded, turning my attention back to the tablet. As I scrolled through, one particular message from Peter caught my eye: "With all this money, we could go live wherever we want. Just say the word, and we'll leave this town behind."

I felt as if all the pieces of the puzzle were suddenly falling into place. The property contract, the cold messages, the plans to leave town – it all painted a picture that was as clear as it was disturbing. I looked at Ginger, and saw the same understanding in his eyes.

"Jim," Ginger said slowly, his voice uncharacteristically serious, "I think we've found our motive."

I nodded, my mind racing with the implications of what we'd discovered. "We need to talk to Maggie. Right now."

"It's midnight," Ginger said. "Unless Maggie's secretly running a 24-hour croissant operation, the bakery's going to be locked up tight."

"Then we'll go to her house," I said, feeling a surge of determination. This mystery had gone on long enough, and it was time to get some answers. "Do you know where she lives?"

Ginger's whiskers twitched, a glimmer of his usual sass returning to his eyes. "As a matter of fact, I do. I make it my business to know where all the best treats in town can be found."

I couldn't help but chuckle at that, despite the seriousness of the situation. Trust Ginger to think with his stomach, even at a time like this.

"Well, Ginger," I said, my voice barely above a whisper, "let's pay a visit to our sweet baker."

I stood up, carefully holding the tablet. As I was about to slip it into my pocket, Ginger spoke up.

"Wait," he said, his tail twitching. "Let me scratch and bite the tablet just a bit."

I blinked in confusion. "Why on earth would you do that?"

Ginger's whiskers twitched in amusement. "How would you explain to the police where you got the tablet? With these scratches and bite marks, you can say a cat probably brought it out of the house and you found it."

"You're quite the criminal mastermind, aren't you?" I said, impressed by Ginger's quick thinking.

After Ginger had left his marks on the tablet, I slipped it into my pocket. It felt heavy, weighted with the secrets it contained. As we made our way out of Peter's house, I took care to leave everything else as we'd found it, erasing any trace of our presence.

The cool night air hit me as we stepped outside, a stark contrast to the stuffy interior of the house. The street was still deserted, the only sound the distant crash of waves against the shore. It amazed me how quickly our fortunes had changed; mere hours ago, we were grasping at straws, and now we held tangible evidence in our hands. It felt like we were standing on the precipice of something big, something that would change Oceanview Cove forever.

The adrenaline coursing through my veins made me feel more alive than I had in years. It was as if I'd been sleepwalking through life since Martha's death, and this mystery had finally woken me up. Despite the gravity of the situation, I couldn't help but feel a spark of excitement.

"You know, Ginger," I chuckled quietly, "I never thought I'd say this, but I'm almost enjoying this detective work."

Ginger snorted, his tail swishing in amusement. "Don't get too excited, old man. We're not out of the woods yet. Remember, if Maggie is involved in Peter's death, she could be dangerous."

His words sobered me quickly. He was right, of course. We were potentially walking into a dangerous situation. Maggie, with her sweet smile and delicious pastries, might be capable of far more than we'd initially thought.

As we approached my house, the streetlights casting long shadows across the pavement, something caught my eye. A figure was moving down the street, walking towards us with purposeful strides. My heart leapt into my throat as recognition dawned.

"Ginger," I whispered, my voice barely audible, "is that who I think it is?"

Ginger's fur bristled, his eyes narrowing as he peered into the darkness. "It's Maggie," he confirmed, his voice tense.

We froze in our tracks, watching as Maggie drew closer, her face hidden in shadow. What was she doing here at this hour? Had she somehow discovered our investigation?

As she neared, the weight of the tablet in my pocket seemed to grow heavier. We were about to come face-to-face with our prime suspect, and I had a sinking feeling that this encounter was about to change everything.

Chapter 17

As Maggie neared, the streetlight illuminated her face, revealing a disheveled appearance that was a far cry from her usual perfectly coiffed look. Her hair was a mess, clothes wrinkled as if hastily thrown on, and her eyes held a wild, almost frantic look. I felt a chill run down my spine. This was not the friendly baker I thought I knew.

"Jim!" she called out, her voice cracking slightly. "Oh, thank goodness I found you. I... I couldn't sleep. Peter and Ryan's deaths, they've upset me so much. They were my friends, you know?"

I exchanged a quick glance with Ginger, whose whiskers twitched in what I'd come to recognize as his skeptical expression. My mind raced, trying to decide how to handle this unexpected encounter. Should I confront her now? Or play along and see what she was up to?

"Maggie," I said, trying to keep my voice steady, "what are you doing out here at this hour?"

She wrung her hands, her eyes darting around nervously. "I just... I needed to talk to someone. You've been so kind since you moved here, and I thought... maybe we could talk? Have a few drinks? I brought some wine." She gestured to a bottle I hadn't noticed before, clutched tightly in her left hand.

I hesitated, my mind racing. This could be a trap, I knew. But confronting her on my home ground seemed safer than our original plan of going to her house. Plus, I had Ginger with me. My feline partner might not look like much, but he'd proven himself invaluable time and time again.

"Of course, Maggie," I said, forcing a smile. "I couldn't sleep either. Just got back from a night walk with Ginger here. Why don't you come in? We can talk at my place."

Relief flooded her features, though I noticed it didn't quite reach her eyes. "Oh, thank you, Jim. You're so kind."

As we walked up to my house, the crunch of gravel under our feet seemed unnaturally loud in the quiet night. Every step felt like we were getting closer to something dangerous, something irreversible. Maggie's eyes darted around, taking in every detail. I couldn't help but wonder if she was looking for escape routes or potential weapons.

"You've done wonders with the place," she said, her voice a little too bright. "It looks so different from when Martha's parents lived here."

I couldn't help but snort at that. "Don't lie, Maggie. I've barely unpacked my belongings, let alone done anything with the place. If anything, it looks worse than when even Martha lived here."

Maggie chuckled, the sound surprisingly genuine. "You're right. I was just trying to be polite, but honesty suits you better, Jim."

As I pushed the door open, I felt a moment of panic. Was I making a terrible mistake inviting her in? But it was too late to back out now. I took a deep breath, trying to calm my racing heart. What would Martha think of me now, inviting a potential murderer into our home? Then again, she'd probably chuckle and tell me I was finally living the detective stories I'd always loved reading. I stepped aside, allowing Maggie to enter first, keeping a watchful eye on her every move. The familiar scent of her bakery – sugar and cinnamon – wafted past me, incongruously sweet in this tense moment. I glanced down at Ginger, drawing strength from his steady presence. Whatever happened next, at least I wasn't facing it alone.

We entered the living room, the cozy space now feeling charged with an undercurrent of tension. The soft glow of the lamp cast warm shadows across the room, but they did little to dispel the chill that had settled in my bones. Maggie sank onto the couch, her posture rigid despite the soft cushions. I took the armchair opposite her, while Ginger positioned himself on the coffee table, his green eyes never leaving Maggie.

"So," I said, breaking the awkward silence. "You wanted to talk?"

Maggie nodded, her eyes welling up with tears. "It's just... Peter and Ryan. I can't believe they're gone. They were such good friends, you know? Peter, he was... he was special to me."

I watched as she dabbed at her eyes with a tissue, her shoulders shaking with what appeared to be genuine sobs. But after what we'd discovered tonight, I couldn't trust anything at face value anymore. Was this all an act? Or was there a glimmer of real emotion behind her tears?

"I understand," I said softly, deciding to play along for now. "Losing friends is never easy. Would you like some tea? It might help calm your nerves."

Maggie nodded gratefully. "That would be lovely, thank you."

As I busied myself in the kitchen, I could hear Ginger's quiet footsteps as he followed me. "Keep your guard up, old man," he murmured. "Something's not right here."

I nodded almost imperceptibly as I filled the kettle. My hands shook slightly as I prepared the tea, my mind whirling with possible scenarios. What if Maggie was here to silence me? What if she knew about our investigation? The weight of Peter's tablet in my pocket seemed to grow heavier with each passing moment. Realizing the importance of this evidence, I made a split-second decision and quickly slipped the tablet behind the cookie jar on the top shelf of a cabinet. It wasn't the most sophisticated hiding place, but it would have to do. I couldn't risk Maggie finding it or, worse, taking it if things went south. With the tablet safely hidden, I turned back to the tea preparation, trying to steady my nerves and appear as normal as possible.

When I returned with two steaming mugs, Maggie had composed herself somewhat, though her hands still trembled slightly as she accepted the tea. I couldn't help but notice how her eyes darted around the room, as if searching for something. Could she be looking for the tablet I'd just hidden?

"You know," I said, settling back into my chair, "I've been meaning to ask you about the bakery. How did you get started in that line of work?"

For the next few minutes, we engaged in light conversation about Maggie's background, her love for baking, and her early days in Oceanview Cove. It was almost possible to forget the real reason for this late-night meeting. Almost. But beneath the veneer of normalcy, I could sense a growing tension, like a rubber band stretched to its limit, ready to snap at any moment.

As our tea cooled, I decided it was time to steer the conversation in a more pointed direction. "Maggie," I began carefully, "you mentioned before that you and Peter had a history. I was wondering if you could tell me more about that."

Maggie's smile faltered slightly, but she quickly regained her composure. "Oh, Jim, I thought we'd already covered this. It was just a brief thing, years ago. Ancient history, really."

I nodded, keeping my tone casual. "Of course, of course. It's just that... well, I've heard some interesting things lately. About you and Peter having some more recent connections."

Maggie's brow furrowed in what appeared to be genuine confusion. "Recent connections? I'm not sure what you mean, Jim. Peter and I remained close after our brief relationship, but it was nothing more than that. We were just friends."

I took a deep breath, deciding to take the plunge. "What about co-owning his house, Maggie? That seems like more than just a friendship."

For a moment, Maggie's face remained blank. Then, slowly, her eyes widened. "Co-owning? Jim, I think there's been some misunderstanding. I don't know anything about—"

"Oh boy, here we go," Ginger muttered, his tail twitching in anticipation. "The cookie's about to crumble."

I leaned forward, my gaze locked on Maggie. "I know about the contract, Maggie. I know about the messages, the plans to sell the house and leave town."

Maggie's composure wavered, but she made one last attempt to deflect. "Jim, I don't know where you're getting this information, but—"

"Maggie," I interrupted gently, "please. I have evidence. It's time for the truth."

Finally, Maggie's carefully constructed facade began to crack. "You don't understand," she whispered, her voice trembling. "Someone's trying to frame me. I would never hurt Peter. Never!"

"Frame you?" I pressed. "Who would want to do that? And why?"

Maggie hesitated, then seemed to make a decision. "It was Ryan," she blurted out, her words tumbling over each other. "He... he was blackmailing me. Forced me to go along with this real estate scheme. But I swear, I didn't know he was going to kill Peter. You have to believe me, Jim!"

I sat back, studying her carefully. Her story sounded plausible, but something didn't quite add up. The desperation in her voice seemed real, but was it desperation born of innocence or guilt?

"Why don't we have a drink?" I suggested, gesturing to the bottle she'd brought. "We can talk this through calmly."

Maggie nodded eagerly, relief evident on her face. As I went to fetch glasses, I could feel the weight of the situation pressing down on me. The cozy living room, once a sanctuary, now felt like a stage set for a tragic play. Every object seemed to hold a potential threat – the heavy paperweight on the side table, the fireplace poker leaning against the wall. I shook my head, trying to dispel these paranoid thoughts.

Returning with the glasses, I poured a generous amount for Maggie and a smaller one for myself. As she sipped her wine, I continued my gentle interrogation.

"So, Ryan was blackmailing you," I said. "What did he have on you?"

Maggie's eyes darted around the room, avoiding my gaze. "He... he knew about some financial irregularities at the bakery. Nothing major, just some... creative accounting. But it would have ruined me if it got out."

I nodded sympathetically, even as my suspicion grew. "And Peter? How did he fit into all this?"

"Peter was innocent," Maggie insisted, her voice cracking. "He didn't know anything about Ryan's scheme. Ryan... Ryan poisoned him. Some kind of rat poison, I think. Slipped it into his drink when they were having beers together, right after you left Peter's house that night."

I froze, my glass halfway to my lips. How did Maggie know about the rat poison? That detail hadn't been made public. In fact, I distinctly remembered Sheriff Miller being very careful with his words during my interrogation. He had only mentioned "poison" in general terms, never specifying the type. The only time he'd come close to revealing more was when he said the traces on my handkerchief were "inconsistent with the type of rat poison that killed Mr. Johnson."

My mind raced, trying to piece together how Maggie could have come across this specific information. Unless... Unless she was more involved than she was letting on. My eyes met Ginger's, and I saw the same realization dawning in his feline features. His tail twitched nervously, a silent signal that we were onto something big. The weight of this revelation settled in my stomach like a lead ball, and I carefully set my glass down, not trusting my suddenly shaky hands.

"Rat poison?" I repeated. "That's an oddly specific detail, Maggie. How did you know that?"

Maggie's face paled, her eyes widening in panic. "I... I must have overheard the police talking about it. Or maybe Ryan mentioned it. I don't remember exactly."

"Or maybe," I said, my voice hard, "it's because you're the one who bought it."

Ginger chose that moment to pounce onto Maggie's handbag, which she'd left on the floor beside her chair. With practiced efficiency, he nudged the bag open with his nose and, in a flash, retrieved a small glass vial, clenching it between his teeth. I felt my own breath catch in my throat as I realized what Ginger had found.

"What... what is that?" Maggie stammered, her face draining of color.

"I believe," I said, standing up slowly, "that's the rat poison you used to kill Peter. The same poison you were planning to use on me tonight."

For a moment, the room was silent, the tension so thick you could cut it with a knife. The only sound was the gentle ticking of the old clock, each second stretching out like an eternity. Maggie's eyes darted between me, Ginger, and the undeniable vial in his mouth, her chest rising and falling rapidly with panicked breaths.

Then, like a dam breaking, Maggie's carefully constructed facade crumbled completely. Her shoulders sagged, the fight visibly draining out of her. The sweet, cheerful baker I thought I knew vanished, replaced by a stranger whose eyes now held a coldness that sent a chill down my spine.

She laughed, a high, almost hysterical sound. "Oh, bravo, Jim. Bravo! I have to hand it to you, you're sharper than I gave you credit for. And your cat... well, he's something else entirely, isn't he?"

"Why, Maggie?" I asked, my voice tight with anger and disappointment. "Why kill Peter? Why frame Ryan?"

Maggie's eyes gleamed with a manic light. "Why? Because I deserved more! I've slaved away in that bakery for years, watching everyone else get ahead while I was stuck in the same old routine. When Peter told me about the developer's offer, I saw my chance."

"So you decided to take matters into your own hands," I finished for her.

She nodded, a cruel smile twisting her lips. "It was almost too easy. I dropped hints that I wanted to get back together with Peter, but only if he sold the house and we left town together. The fool was so eager to please, he practically begged me to be co-owner of the house. Once that was done, killing him was the next logical step."

"And Ryan? Where does he fit into all this?" I asked, my stomach churning.

Maggie laughed, a cold, hollow sound. "Ryan was perfect, so easy to manipulate. I promised him a cut of the money if he helped me. He even volunteered to do the deed himself, can you believe it? After you left Peter's house looking so upset, Ryan saw his chance. Went over to 'comfort' his neighbor, and slipped the poison into Peter's drink."

I felt sick. "And Ryan's death? That was you too, wasn't it?"

"Of course," Maggie said, her voice casual. "He knew too much, was getting nervous. It was simple enough to stage his suicide. I hadn't planned on that ridiculous confession note, but when the police released you, I had to act fast. I thought that would be the end of it."

Her eyes narrowed as she looked at me. "But you just couldn't leave well enough alone, could you? You had to keep digging, keep asking questions. When I saw Peter's Messenger account go online tonight, I knew you'd somehow found his tablet and discovered the truth. I couldn't let that stand."

A thought struck me. "What about my handkerchief? The one found with traces of poison?"

Maggie's lips curled into a smirk. "Ah, that. You really should be more careful with your belongings, Jim. You left it at the bakery during your first visit. I saw an opportunity and took it. It was supposed to be the final nail in your coffin, but I made a miscalculation."

"The wrong type of rat poison," I guessed.

She nodded. "I didn't realize Ryan had used a different brand until I went to kill him and found the evidence. By then, it was too late. The police had already released you."

"And the knife?" I pressed. "Robert's knife that we found near the police station?"

"Another of Ryan's bright ideas," Maggie scoffed. "He had it as a backup plan, in case the police released you. Thought it would point suspicion back to Robert. It worked out well for me, though. While you were busy chasing that red herring, I was able to take care of Ryan without any interference."

As the full extent of Maggie's deception unfolded, I felt a mix of horror and anger rising within me. This woman, who I'd thought was just a friendly baker, had orchestrated two murders and attempted to frame me for one of them. The weight of it all settled in my chest like a cold, heavy stone. I thought of Peter, who had loved her enough to make her co-owner of his house, and of Ryan, manipulated into becoming an unwitting accomplice. Both of them had trusted Maggie, just as I had. I recalled my two visits to her bakery – that first time enjoying her croissants and coffee, and the second when I'd gone to question her. How easily she had played the part of the sweet, unassuming baker, never betraying the darkness that lurked behind her cheerful facade. The pleasant aroma of baked goods that I'd enjoyed on those visits now seemed sickening. I couldn't help but wonder if any part of her friendly demeanor had been genuine. A chill ran down my spine as

I realized the gravity of my situation. This woman had already proven herself capable of murder, and now, she was here to silence me permanently.

"So you came here to kill me," I said, the realization hitting me like a punch to the gut.

Maggie stood up slowly, her hand reaching into her pocket. "That was the plan. Still is, as a matter of fact."

In a flash, she pulled out a pair of gloves and quickly slipped them on. Before I could react, she lunged at me, her hands outstretched towards my throat.

I stumbled backward, nearly tripping over my own feet in my haste to get away. But Maggie was surprisingly quick for a baker. Her fingers closed around my neck, squeezing with a strength born of desperation.

The room began to spin as I struggled for air. Maggie's face, contorted with rage and determination, filled my vision. I clawed at her hands, trying to break her grip, but she held on with the strength of a madwoman.

Just as spots began to dance in my vision, I heard a yowl that would have done a banshee proud. Ginger launched himself at Maggie's face, claws extended and teeth bared.

Maggie screamed, more in surprise than pain, and staggered backward. Her grip on my throat loosened as she tried to pry Ginger off her face. I gasped for air, my lungs burning as I sucked in precious oxygen.

In the scuffle, one of her gloves came off, fluttering to the floor. Ginger's claws had left red scratches across her cheek, drawing blood.

"You mangy fleabag!" she shrieked, finally managing to dislodge Ginger and toss him aside.

I lunged for the fireplace poker, brandishing it like a weapon. "It's over, Maggie," I wheezed, my voice hoarse from the attack. "Give yourself up."

But Maggie, nursing the wounds from Ginger's attack and realizing her plan had failed, made a desperate dash for the door. "This isn't over, Jim!" she yelled as she yanked it open. "You'll regret this!"

As she disappeared into the night, I staggered to the door, still gasping for breath. Ginger was at my side in an instant, his fur bristling with agitation.

"Are you okay, Ginger?" I asked. "She didn't hurt you, did she?"

Ginger shook his head impatiently. "I'm fine, old man. We can't let her get away," he hissed. "She's desperate now, and a desperate Maggie is a dangerous Maggie."

I nodded, my mind racing. We couldn't wait for the police. By the time they arrived, Maggie could be long gone.

"Go after her, Ginger," I said, my voice raspy but filled with determination. "I'll be right behind you. Don't let her out of your sight!"

Ginger nodded, his green eyes gleaming with fierce resolve. Without another word, he shot out the open door, his orange fur soon swallowed by the darkness.

I paused only long enough to grab my cell phone. As I stepped out into the cool night air, I could hear the distant sound of Ginger's paws pounding on the pavement. The gravity of what had just happened hit me like a tidal wave. We had uncovered the truth, but our night was far from over. We had a cunning baker to catch.

Chapter 18

I ran out into the street, my shoes slapping against the sidewalk as I followed Ginger's lead. The adrenaline from my encounter with Maggie was still coursing through my veins, but my body – unused to such exertion – was already protesting. Ahead of me, Ginger's orange fur was a barely visible streak in the darkness, his paws pounding the pavement with determined urgency.

"Ginger!" I wheezed, trying to keep up. "Which way did she go?"

The weight of responsibility pressed down on me – I had to stop Maggie, to prevent her from hurting anyone else or escaping justice.

"Towards the waterfront!" Ginger's voice floated back to me. "Hurry, old man! She's faster than she looks!"

I pushed myself harder, ignoring the burning in my legs and the stitch forming in my side. The quiet streets of Oceanview Cove, usually so peaceful at this hour, now echoed with the sound of our pursuit.

As we neared the waterfront, the salty tang of the sea filled my nostrils, mixing with the coppery taste of exertion in my mouth. My lungs felt like they were on fire, and I silently cursed my sedentary lifestyle. Who knew retirement would involve so much running?

Suddenly, Ginger skidded to a halt at an intersection, his tail swishing in agitation. "I've lost her scent," he hissed, frustration evident in his voice.

I leaned against a lamppost, trying to catch my breath. My heart was pounding so hard I feared it might burst out of my chest. "She... she must be heading for the docks," I panted, my mind working overtime despite my physical exhaustion. "It's... the only way out of town at this hour."

Ginger nodded, his green eyes glowing in the dim light. "You're right. Come on, we can cut through the alley here. It'll save us some time."

We plunged into the narrow passage between two buildings, the darkness enveloping us. I stumbled over unseen obstacles, my hand trailing along the rough brick wall for guidance. The alley seemed to stretch on forever, the sounds of the sea growing tantalizingly closer with each step. But what if we were too late? What if Maggie had already escaped?

Finally, we burst out onto the waterfront. The docks sprawled before us, a maze of weathered wooden planks and gently bobbing boats. The sky was just beginning to lighten, the first hints of dawn painting the horizon in soft pinks and oranges. But there was no time to appreciate the beauty of the scene.

"There!" Ginger yowled, his ears pricked forward. "By the fishing boats!"

I squinted in the direction he indicated, my tired eyes struggling to focus in the dim light. And then I saw her – a figure darting between the moored vessels. Maggie's blonde hair, usually so perfectly styled, was a wild tangle streaming behind her as she ran. The sight of her filled me with a mix of anger and determination. After everything she'd done, I couldn't let her get away.

"Maggie!" I shouted, my voice hoarse and cracking. "Stop! It's over!"

She glanced back, her eyes wide with panic, and redoubled her efforts. I watched in horror as she leaped into a small rowboat, her hands fumbling with the oars. The reality of the situation hit me like a punch to the gut – if she made it out to open water, we'd never catch her.

"No!" I gasped, pushing my protesting body into a final sprint. "Ginger, we can't let her get away!"

But Ginger was already ahead of me, a streak of orange fur flying across the dock. With a mighty leap he soared through the air and landed in Maggie's boat just as she pushed off from the dock.

Maggie screamed as Ginger's claws dug into her arm, causing her to drop one of the oars. The boat veered wildly, nearly capsizing as it drifted away from the dock. My heart leaped into my throat as I watched the small boat rock dangerously. If it capsized, would Ginger be able to swim to safety?

I skidded to a halt at the water's edge, my heart pounding. "Ginger!" I called out, fear for my feline friend overriding everything else.

But Ginger was holding his own. He was a blur of fur and claws, scratching and biting at Maggie as she tried desperately to shake him off and control the boat at the same time. Their struggle was a chaotic dance, the small boat pitching and rolling with each movement.

I looked around frantically, my eyes landing on another small boat tied nearby. Without thinking, I jumped in, my fingers fumbling with the knot. The rope seemed to fight against me, each second feeling like an eternity as Maggie's boat drifted further away. Finally, the knot came loose, and I grabbed the oars, pushing off from the dock with all my strength.

"Hold on, Ginger!" I shouted, my arms straining as I rowed. "I'm coming!"

The two boats weaved a chaotic path across the harbor, Maggie's erratic steering a result of her battle with Ginger. I rowed harder than I ever had in my life, the muscles in my arms and back screaming in protest. Each stroke felt like it might be my last, but I pushed through the pain, driven by the need to stop Maggie and save Ginger.

Slowly, agonizingly, I began to close the distance. Maggie's boat, out of control with only one oar, was circling back towards me. I adjusted my course, trying to anticipate where they would end up. The sound of splashing water and desperate shouts filled my ears, punctuated by Ginger's fierce yowls.

As the gap narrowed, I could make out Maggie's face, her features contorted with fury. They were close now, so close I could hear Maggie's labored breathing and Ginger's angry hisses.

Suddenly, Maggie managed to get a grip on Ginger. With a strength born of desperation, she lifted him and tossed him overboard. "Ginger!" I yelled, watching in horror as my friend disappeared beneath the water's surface. My heart stopped for a moment, fear for Ginger overwhelming everything else.

In that moment of distraction, Maggie's boat drifted right next to mine. Seizing the opportunity, I stood up in my small vessel, raising one of the oars like a weapon. As Maggie turned to face me, her eyes wild with fear and anger, I hesitated for a split second. This was Maggie, the woman who had welcomed me to town with a warm smile and delicious pastries. But then I remembered Peter and Ryan, their lives cut short by her greed. With grim determination, I swung the oar with all my might.

There was a sickening thud as the oar connected with Maggie's head. Her eyes rolled back, and she fell onto the boat's floor, unconscious. For a moment, I stood there, panting, the reality of what I'd just done washing over me. But there was no time to dwell on it.

"Ginger!" I called out, frantically scanning the water. "Ginger, where are you?" My voice cracked with desperation as I maneuvered my boat closer to where I'd last seen him, my heart in my throat. "Ginger!" I called again, reaching out with my oar, hoping against hope.

For a few terrifying moments, there was nothing. The silence was deafening, broken only by the gentle lapping of waves against the boat. Then, just as despair was about to overwhelm me, I felt a tug on the oar. Ginger's bedraggled head popped up above the water, his paws gripping the oar tightly.

With a strength I didn't know I possessed, I hauled him aboard. Ginger collapsed on the floor of the boat, coughing and sputtering. A wave of relief washed over me as I saw he was alive.

"Oh, Ginger," I breathed, scooping him up and hugging him tightly, not caring about my now-soaked clothes. "I thought I'd lost you." The fear of losing my feline friend, the one constant in this chaotic new life of mine, had been almost unbearable.

Ginger, still catching his breath, managed a weak chuckle. "It'll take more than a dip in the harbor to get rid of me, old man. Though I could do without the crushing hug – I've had enough near-death experiences for one night."

I laughed in relief, loosening my grip but still cradling him close. "Fair enough, my friend. Fair enough."

With Ginger safe, I turned my attention back to Maggie. I quickly tied her hands with my belt, just in case she woke up, and began towing her boat back to the dock. The adrenaline was starting to wear off, and I could feel every ache and pain in my body. But there was a sense of grim satisfaction too – we had done it. We had caught the killer.

As we approached the dock, I could see flashing red and blue lights. Someone must have called the police, likely a neighbor awakened by our chase. Sheriff Miller stood at the edge of the dock, his bulky silhouette unmistakable even from a distance. As we drew closer, I could see his face clearly in the lights of the police vehicles. His expression was a mask of disbelief, his usual air of confident authority replaced by wide-eyed shock as he took in the scene before him.

"Butterfield?" he called out as we reached the pier. "What in the world is going on here?"

I tied up both boats and helped the officers secure Maggie before turning to Miller. Exhaustion hit me like a wave, and I swayed slightly on my feet. "It's a long story, Sheriff. But the short version is, Maggie Brown is your killer."

Miller's eyebrows shot up. "Maggie? The baker? Butterfield, that's a serious accusation. Do you have any proof?"

I nodded, suddenly feeling the weight of the night's events. "All the evidence is back at my house. Peter's tablet is hidden behind the cookie jar in the top cabinet in the kitchen. The password is G-I-N-G-E-R-C-A-T. You'll want to check the messages between Peter and Maggie. The vial of poison and the gloves she used are on the coffee table in the living room. And I'm sure if you search her house and the bakery, you'll find more evidence."

Miller looked skeptical, but nodded to his young officers. "Martinez, go check Mr. Butterfield's house. Bring back anything you find." He turned back to me. "We'll check it out, Butterfield. But I hope for your sake you're right about this."

As we waited for the officer to return, the paramedics tended to Maggie. She began to stir, her eyes fluttering open. As the realization of her situation dawned on her, she began to struggle against her restraints.

"No!" she cried out, her voice hoarse and desperate. "You don't understand! I'm innocent! Butterfield is the one you should be arresting!"

Her pleas fell on deaf ears as the officers helped her to her feet. I watched, a mix of pity and anger swirling in my chest. How had things come to this?

The docks began to fill with early-rising fishermen, drawn by the commotion. They gathered in small groups, whispering and pointing, no doubt already spreading the story of how the new guy in town – the retired librarian, of all people – had been involved in a dramatic boat chase.

I caught snippets of their conversations as they prepared their boats for the day's work:

"Can you believe it? Old Jim Butterfield, chasing down Maggie Brown?"

"I always said there was something off about that woman. Nobody's croissants are that good without some kind of dark secret."

"Wonder what really happened to Peter and Ryan? Guess we'll find out soon enough."

Their words filled me with a strange mix of anticipation and dread. The truth would come out now, but at what cost to this small community?

As the sun finally appeared on the horizon, bathing the harbor in golden light, I found myself standing at the edge of the dock, Ginger by my side. We watched as Maggie, still protesting her innocence, was led to a police car. Her eyes met mine for a moment, filled with a mixture of hatred and something that might have been respect.

"You know, Ginger," I said softly, "when I moved here, I was looking for a quiet place to retire. To escape the excitement of the city and settle into a peaceful routine."

Ginger snorted, a very un-catlike sound. "Well, old man, I'd say you failed spectacularly at that."

I chuckled, reaching down to scratch behind his ears. "That I did, my friend. That I did."

Just then, the officer returned from my house, carrying an evidence bag. "Sheriff," he called out, "you're going to want to see this."

Miller examined the contents of the bag – the tablet, the vial, and the gloves. His eyes widened as he scrolled through the messages on the tablet. "Well, I'll be," he muttered. He looked up at me, a newfound respect in his eyes. "Looks like you were right, Butterfield. We'll need to go over everything in detail, but this... this is pretty incriminating evidence."

I nodded, feeling a weight lift off my shoulders. "I'm just glad it's over, Sheriff."

Miller approached us, his face serious. "Butterfield, I owe you an apology. I was so sure you were involved, I couldn't see what was right in front of me. You've done this town a great service."

"We all make mistakes, Sheriff," I said, too tired to hold onto any resentment. "The important thing is that the truth came out in the end."

"Speaking of the truth," Miller said, "Butterfield, I'm going to need you to come down to the station. We need to go over everything, and I mean everything. No detail is too small."

I nodded, feeling the exhaustion of the night finally catching up with me. "Of course, Sheriff. But first, I think I need a cup of coffee and a dry set of clothes."

Miller cracked a small smile. "I think we can arrange that. And Butterfield? Good work tonight. Even if I'm not entirely sure what 'good work' entails in this case."

As Miller walked away, I couldn't help but marvel at the twists and turns my life had taken. From a quiet librarian to an amateur detective, from a lonely widower to a man with an extraordinary feline friend.

The sun climbed higher in the sky, its warmth chasing away the last of the night's chill. Oceanview Cove was waking up to a new day, one that would undoubtedly be filled with revelations and hard truths.

Chapter 19

The Oceanview Cove police station was a hive of activity. The air hummed with tension and excitement, punctuated by the occasional ring of a telephone or the click of computer keys. I sat in an uncomfortable plastic chair, my clothes still damp from the earlier chase in the harbor, with Ginger curled up at my feet.

Sheriff Miller emerged from his office, his face a mask of professional detachment. "Alright, Mr. Butterfield. We need your full statement now."

I nodded, standing up. Ginger stretched and made to follow, but Miller held up a hand. "Not the cat. He'll have to wait outside."

"I'm not going anywhere without Ginger," I said firmly, surprising myself with my boldness. "He's as much a part of this as I am."

Miller's mustache twitched in annoyance. "This isn't a petting zoo, Butterfield. It's a police station."

Ginger chose that moment to let out a particularly disgruntled hiss. I couldn't help but smile at his perfect timing.

"Look," I said, "Ginger's been through a lot tonight. He nearly drowned helping me catch Maggie. I'm not leaving him alone."

Miller sighed, pinching the bridge of his nose. "Rules are rules, Butterfield. We'll put him in the pet room while you give your statement. It's warm, and there's water and some cat food."

Ginger let out an indignant meow, "Pet room? Do I look like some common house cat to you? I'm a detective, for crying out loud!"

I knelt down to Ginger's level. "It won't take long, I promise. Why don't you let the officer take you to the pet room? I'll be done before you know it."

Ginger's tail twitched in annoyance, but he finally relented. "Fine," he meowed. "As long as they have decent cat food. None of that dry kibble nonsense."

I stood up and nodded to Miller. "He'll go to the pet room. But please make sure he's comfortable. He's earned it after tonight."

Miller nodded, gesturing for an officer to take Ginger. As Ginger was led away, I couldn't help but feel a twinge of separation anxiety. But I knew I had a job to finish. It was time to give my statement and bring this case to a close.

As I followed Miller to the interrogation room, I couldn't help but marvel at the surreal turn my life had taken. Just a few weeks ago, I was a lonely retiree, and now here I was, about to give a statement about solving a double homicide. Life certainly had a way of surprising you.

The next few hours passed in a blur of questions and answers. I recounted every detail, from my first meeting with Peter to the dramatic boat chase with Maggie. Miller listened intently, his pen scratching across his notepad as he documented my story. Occasionally, he'd interject with a question or ask for clarification, but for the most part, he let me talk uninterrupted.

By the time we finished, sunlight was streaming through the station's windows. I felt exhausted but relieved, like I'd finally set down a heavy burden I'd been carrying for weeks.

"Well, Butterfield," Miller said, leaning back in his chair, "I've got to hand it to you. You've done some fine detective work here. Though I still can't quite believe it was Maggie all along."

I nodded, understanding his disbelief. "Believe me, Sheriff, I'm still having trouble wrapping my head around it myself."

As we stepped out of the interrogation room, a young officer approached Miller, his face flushed with excitement. "Sheriff, you need to see this. We've found more evidence at Ryan's house and in Maggie's phone."

Miller's eyebrows shot up. "What kind of evidence?"

"A receipt for rat poison in Ryan's trash, dated the day before Peter's death. And messages between Maggie and

Ryan on her phone that corroborate everything Mr. Butterfield told us."

I felt a wave of relief wash over me. It was one thing for Miller to believe my story, but hard evidence would make it impossible for anyone to doubt the truth.

Miller nodded, clearly impressed. "Good work. Anything else?"

The young officer hesitated, then added, "Yes, sir. The gloves we found in Maggie's possession? They have traces of Ryan's DNA on them. It looks like she used them to stage his suicide and then planned to use them on Mr. Butterfield."

I shuddered at the thought of how close I'd come to being Maggie's third victim. Miller noticed my discomfort and placed a hand on my shoulder. "You did good, Butterfield. You brought a killer to justice and saved your own life in the process."

As we made our way to the front of the station to collect Ginger, the buzz of voices from outside caught my attention. Miller frowned, moving to the window. "What in the world?"

I joined him, peering out onto the street. A crowd had gathered outside the station, their faces a mix of curiosity and concern. I recognized some of them – Emma the astrologer, her colorful scarves fluttering in the breeze; Shawn the bartender, his usually cheery face creased with worry; Robert Reeves, the fisherman, standing off to the side with his arms crossed.

"Looks like word's gotten out," I murmured.

Miller sighed heavily. "I suppose it was bound to happen in a town this size. Stay here, Butterfield. I'll go talk to them."

But as Miller stepped outside, the crowd's murmurs grew louder, more insistent. I could see Miller trying to calm them down, but his words seemed to have little effect. Making a split-second decision, I went to retrieve Ginger from the pet room.

As I opened the door, Ginger bounded out, looking relieved to see me.

"How was it?" I asked quietly, kneeling down to his level.

Ginger's tail twitched in annoyance. "Awful," he meowed. "The food tasted like cardboard, and the other cats were about as intelligent as lint. No one to hold a decent conversation with."

I chuckled softly. "Well, it's over now. Ready to face the crowds?"

Ginger's whiskers twitched. "As long as we're not going back in there, I'm ready for anything."

With Ginger by my side, I joined Miller outside the station.

The morning sun was bright, making me squint as I stepped onto the station's front steps. The crowd fell silent as they noticed me and Ginger, all eyes turning in our direction.

"Sheriff," I said quietly, "they won't calm down until they get some answers."

Miller looked at me for a long moment, then nodded. "Alright, Butterfield. You've earned the right to tell this story. But keep it brief, understand?"

I nodded, then turned to face the crowd. Taking a deep breath, I began to speak.

"Friends, neighbors, I know you're all wondering what in the world is going on. Trust me, I'm still trying to wrap my head around it myself. These past few days have turned our quiet little town upside down, haven't they? Two of our neighbors gone, a midnight chase in the harbor, and now Maggie in handcuffs. It's a lot to process, I know. But if you'll bear with me for a few minutes, I'll do my best to explain what really happened here.

"It all started with Peter's house. He was planning to sell it to a developer who wanted to turn it into a bed and breakfast. Maggie saw this as an opportunity to make a quick fortune. She manipulated Peter into making her co-owner of the house, playing on his old feelings for her. But she didn't stop there. Her plan was to kill Peter, take all the money from the sale for herself, and then leave town. She wanted the whole pie, not just half.

"But Maggie didn't act alone. She manipulated Ryan too, promising him a cut of the money if he helped her. Ryan was the one who actually poisoned Peter, using rat poison that we now have evidence he purchased the day before Peter's death. Ryan didn't know the full extent of

Maggie's plan at first. By the time he realized what he'd done, it was too late.

"Maggie, fearing that Ryan might confess and not wanting to split the money with him, decided to silence him permanently. She used the gloves to strangle Ryan, and then staged his death to look like a suicide. These same gloves, which we've now found contain traces of Ryan's DNA, were the ones she intended to use on me when she came to my house last night. Her plan was to eliminate the last person who could expose her crimes. Maggie was determined to keep all the money from the house sale for herself, leaving no loose ends or anyone to share the profits with."

I paused, letting the weight of my words sink in. The crowd was silent, their faces a mix of shock and disbelief. Some shook their heads, others whispered to their neighbors, and a few even dabbed at their eyes with handkerchiefs.

I could see the pain of betrayal etched on their features. Maggie, the sweet baker who'd been a fixture in their lives, whose croissants had been a staple of their mornings, was now revealed as a cold-blooded killer. It was a lot to take in, and I felt the weight of their shock and sorrow as if it were my own.

Ginger, sitting at my feet, let out a soft meow. "Don't forget to mention the dashing feline detective who made all this possible, old man."

Suppressing a smile, I continued, "Now, I know you're wondering how I uncovered all of this. The truth is, I had help. Ginger here," I gestured to my feline partner, "was actually Peter's cat before. One night, he snuck into Peter's house and, while playing around, found a hidden tablet. For some reason, Ginger brought it to my front door. I don't know why he did that, but it turned out to be crucial evidence. That tablet contained messages between Peter and Maggie that revealed their plans to sell the house. And last night, Ginger helped me stop Maggie when she tried to escape, even jumping into her boat to slow her down."

At this, Ginger puffed up his chest proudly, earning a few chuckles from the crowd.

As I finished speaking, a hush fell over the gathered townspeople. Then, the questions began.

Shawn, the bartender, spoke up first. "But Jim, how did you manage to unlock Peter's tablet?"

"It was a hunch, really," I explained. "I remembered Peter saying how much he loved Ginger, so I guessed he might have used Ginger's name as a password. Turns out, I was right."

Dorie, the silver-haired cashier who had helped me at the quaint little market on my first day here, raised her hand. "And what about Ryan? How did you figure out he was involved?"

I nodded, acknowledging her question. "At first, Maggie told me about Ryan's involvement when she came to my house, thinking she could silence me. Later, when the police found messages between Ryan and Maggie on her phone, it confirmed everything."

"But why didn't the police find all this evidence?" Robert Reeves asked, eyeing Sheriff Miller suspiciously.

Miller cleared his throat awkwardly. "We were... in the process of investigating. These things take time."

Ginger let out a noise that sounded like a snort, "Yeah, right. They couldn't find their own badges if they weren't pinned to their chests."

I quickly continued, hoping to smooth over the awkward moment. "I know this is a lot to take in, but the important thing is that the truth has come out. The true killer has been caught, and she'll answer for what she's done. This has been a dark chapter for our town, but we'll get through this, together. And who knows? We might just come out stronger on the other side."

The crowd fell silent as I finished speaking. Then, slowly, a smattering of applause began, growing louder until it echoed off the buildings around us. I felt my face flush with embarrassment at the unexpected show of appreciation.

Emma pushed her way to the front of the crowd, her eyes shining with unshed tears. "Jim, my dear, the stars told me you would bring great change to our town, but I never imagined this. You truly are a remarkable man."

Ginger snorted. "I thought she only predicted trouble for you, old man. Looks like her crystal ball needs recalibrating."

Shawn stepped forward next, clapping me on the shoulder. "You've done us all a great service, Jim. How about we celebrate properly? Drinks at the Salty Breeze, on the house!"

The crowd cheered at this suggestion, but I hesitated. The events of the past few days were catching up with me, and I felt bone-tired. "I appreciate the offer, Shawn, but I think I need to get some sleep."

Shawn's face fell slightly, but then he grinned. "Come on, Jim. Just for a little while. I'll make you that Librarian cocktail you liked so much. It won't take long, I promise."

I looked down at Ginger, he nodded and said, "You've earned it, old man. Besides, I wouldn't mind a saucer of cream myself."

"Well," I said to Shawn, a smile tugging at my lips, "when you put it that way, how can I refuse?"

The crowd cheered again, and we began to make our way towards the Salty Breeze. As we walked, I felt a sense of belonging I hadn't experienced since Martha's death. These people, this town – they had become more than just a place to retire. They had become home.

Ginger trotted beside me, his tail held high. "You know," I said quietly to him, "I couldn't have done any of this without you."

He looked up at me, his green eyes glinting with amusement. "Of course you couldn't," he seemed to say. "Someone had to keep you out of trouble. Though I have to say, for a human, you didn't do too badly."

As we strolled down the street in the direction of the Salty Breeze, the morning sun warming my back and the sounds of chatter filling the air, I couldn't help but feel a mix of emotions. Relief that the case was solved, sadness for the lives lost, and a touch of excitement for what the future might hold.

Chapter 20

The walk to the Salty Breeze felt like a parade. Shawn led the way, his usual jovial demeanor amplified by excitement. Emma fluttered alongside, her colorful scarves dancing in the sea breeze. A crowd of townsfolk followed, their chatter filling the air with a buzz of anticipation. Ginger and I found ourselves at the center of this impromptu procession, still somewhat dazed by the turn of events.

"You know," Ginger muttered, his voice audible only to me, "for a quiet seaside town, these people sure know how to make a fuss."

I chuckled, earning curious glances from those nearby. "Just wait until we get to the bar," I whispered back. "I have a feeling it's only going to get louder."

As we approached the Salty Breeze, Shawn threw open the doors with a flourish. "Ladies and gentlemen," he announced, his voice carrying over the murmur of the crowd, "I present to you the heroes of Oceanview Cove!"

A cheer went up as we stepped inside, the usually quiet bar now thrumming with excited energy. The air was thick with the scent of beer and the tang of celebratory spirits. It was a far cry from the hushed whispers and suspicious glances of just a few days ago.

"First round's on the house!" Shawn called out as he made his way behind the bar. "In fact, all drinks are on the house today! We're celebrating our town's heroes!"

Another cheer erupted, and I found myself being ushered onto a barstool, Ginger leaping gracefully onto the one beside me.

"Here you go, Jim," Shawn said, sliding a familiar-looking cocktail in front of me. "One Librarian, as promised."

I took a sip, savoring the complex flavors. "Delicious, as always."

Shawn winked. "Well, I'd hope so. Can't have our local celebrity drinking subpar cocktails, now can we?"

"Local celebrity," I scoffed. "I'm just a retired librarian who got lucky."

"Luck, he says," Ginger snorted, lapping at a saucer of cream Shawn had placed before him. "As if I didn't do all the heavy lifting."

I stifled a laugh, covering it with a cough as Emma settled into the seat next to Ginger.

"The stars aligned perfectly for you, Jim," she said, her eyes twinkling. "I knew from the moment you arrived that you were destined for greatness in our little town."

"Oh, here we go with the star talk again," Ginger muttered, pausing from his cream. "I suppose the constellations told her all about my daring boat leap too."

I bit my lip to keep from laughing out loud. "Well, Emma," I managed, "I'm not sure about stars, but I certainly had help." I glanced down at Ginger, who was back to lapping contentedly at his cream. "I couldn't have done it without this guy."

"To Jim and Ginger!" Shawn called out, raising a glass. The entire bar echoed the toast, the sound of clinking glasses filling the air.

As the initial excitement died down, I noticed a familiar gruff figure making his way through the crowd. Robert Reeves settled onto the stool on my other side, nodding a greeting.

Shawn's eyebrows shot up in surprise. "Robert? I didn't expect to see you here. You're not exactly a regular."

Robert shrugged, his weathered face creasing into what might have been a smile. "Couldn't miss this, could I? It's not every day we celebrate a hero in Oceanview Cove. Besides, Jim here returned my lost knife. Figured I owed him a drink."

Shawn's brow furrowed, clearly intrigued. "Your knife? How did Jim end up with that?"

"It's a long story," Robert replied, waving his hand dismissively. He turned to me, raising his glass. "To Jim Butterfield, the man who solved the mystery and saved my favorite filleting knife."

I felt my face flush with embarrassment. "Hero?" I protested, trying to deflect the attention. "I think that's a bit much. I just did what anyone would do."

"Anyone?" Robert snorted. "I don't see anyone else solving mysteries around here."

"Well," Shawn chimed in, a mischievous glint in his eyes, "there was that time Emma solved the great pancake mystery at the Summer Fest. Remember that, Emma?"

Emma huffed indignantly. "I'll have you know, Shawn O'Connell, that was a very precise celestial alignment that led to that revelation!"

Shawn grinned. "Oh, it was very precise. Emma declared the stars told her the missing pancakes were 'in a dark, moist place.' Turns out, they were in Mayor Thompson's stomach. He'd been sneaking them all morning!"

We all burst into laughter, the tension of the past few days finally breaking. Even Ginger seemed amused, his whiskers twitching as he watched our banter.

As our laughter died down, Robert's face grew serious. "So," he said, his voice gruff but curious, "what happens now? To the town, I mean."

I considered his question. "I'm not sure," I admitted. "There's still a lot to sort out. Peter's house, for one thing."

"Ah yes," Emma nodded sagely. "The house that started it all. What will become of it, I wonder?"

Shawn, who had been polishing glasses behind the bar, leaned in. "Well, if Peter signed that contract with the developer, it might still go through. Those things are usually valid even after death."

"Really?" I asked, surprised. "Even with all that's happened?"

Shawn shrugged. "Legal stuff gets complicated. But yeah, it's possible."

"And what about Ryan's place?" Robert asked. "Did he have any family?"

We all looked at Shawn, who seemed to be the unofficial town encyclopedia. He frowned, thinking. "You know, I'm not sure. Ryan was always asking about everyone else's business, but he never talked much about himself."

"Figures," Robert grunted. "Man was nosier than a bloodhound but tighter than a clam about his own life."

I couldn't help but chuckle at the comparison. "Well, I suppose that's something for the lawyers to figure out."

As the afternoon wore on, I felt the weight of the past few days settling on my shoulders. The adrenaline that had kept me going was wearing off, leaving behind a bone-deep exhaustion.

"I hate to cut the celebration short," I said, stifling a yawn, "but I think I need to get some sleep. It's been a long couple of days."

Understanding nods met my announcement. Emma patted my hand. "Of course, dear. You've certainly earned your rest."

"Don't be a stranger," Shawn said as I stood up. "You're always welcome here, both of you." He nodded at Ginger, who had finished his cream and was looking like the cat that ate the canary.

As we made our way out of the bar, more well-wishes and thanks followed us. The warm glow of appreciation stayed with me as we stepped out into the cool evening air.

The walk home was quiet, the excitement of the day giving way to a peaceful calm. The sun was setting over the ocean, turning the sky into a watercolor masterpiece. The gentle lapping of waves against the shore provided a soothing backdrop to our journey.

About halfway home, I remembered my promise to myself to call Sarah once everything was over. I pulled out my phone, Ginger watching curiously as I dialed.

"Dad?" Sarah's voice came through, a mix of surprise and concern. "Is everything okay? You never call this late."

I chuckled. "Everything's fine, sweetheart. Better than fine, actually. But you might want to sit down for this."

Over the next few minutes, I recounted the events of the past few days – the murders, the investigation, and our dramatic capture of Maggie. Sarah's gasps and exclamations punctuated my story.

When I finished, there was a long pause. Then, "Dad, why didn't you call me earlier? I can't believe you went through all that without letting me know!"

I sighed, feeling a twinge of guilt. "I'm sorry, honey. I didn't want to worry you. And to be honest, everything happened so fast, I barely had time to think."

"But still," Sarah protested, "you could have been hurt! Or worse!"

"I know, I know," I said soothingly. "But I'm okay. Really. And I promise, next time I get involved in a murder investigation, you'll be my first call."

There was a beat of silence, then Sarah burst out laughing. "Only you, Dad. Only you could move to a quiet seaside town for retirement and end up solving murders."

I chuckled along with her, feeling the tension dissipate. "Well, all those years of reading mystery novels were bound to pay off someday."

"That's for sure," Sarah agreed. Then her voice softened. "You know, Dad, I was worried when you decided to move to Oceanview Cove. I thought you'd be lonely, or bored. But now... well, I haven't heard you sound this alive in years."

I felt a lump form in my throat. "I know what you mean. I feel more alive than I have since your mother passed. And you know, I've found some real friends here. Good people who've accepted me into their community."

"Mom would be proud of you, Dad," Sarah said. "So am I."

We chatted for a few more minutes, Sarah extracting a promise from me to call more often and to be careful. As I pocketed my phone, I noticed Ginger watching me intently.

"What?" I asked.

Ginger just blinked slowly, then turned to continue walking. But I could have sworn I saw a hint of approval in those green eyes.

As we approached our house, I found myself hesitating. The events of the past few days had awakened something in me, a spark I thought had died with Martha. The thought of going back to a quiet retirement suddenly seemed... less appealing.

"You know, Ginger," I said as we climbed the porch steps, "I'm not sure I'm ready to retire just yet."

Ginger looked up at me, his tail twitching with interest.

"I mean, we make a pretty good team, don't we?" I continued, unlocking the door. "Maybe we could... I don't know, do this more often?"

As we stepped inside, Ginger said, "It's about time you figured that out, old man."

I chuckled, settling into my favorite armchair. Ginger hopped up onto the coffee table, his favorite place for our conversations.

"So, what are you saying?" Ginger asked. "You want to become a full-time detective?"

I shrugged. "Maybe not full-time. But we could open a small agency. Take on cases here and there. What do you think?"

Ginger's whiskers twitched in what I'd come to recognize as his version of a smile. "I think you'd be bored out of your mind without a mystery to solve. Besides, someone has to keep you out of trouble."

We spent the next ten minutes discussing the idea, weighing the pros and cons. As our conversation wound down, I found myself feeling more energized than I had in years.

"You know," I said, an idea suddenly striking me, "we should have a name. For our agency, I mean."

Ginger's ears perked up. "Oh? What did you have in mind?"

I thought for a moment, then smiled. "How about 'The Oceanview Cove Investigators'? Has a nice ring to it, don't you think?"

Ginger seemed to consider this, then nodded his approval. "Not bad, old man. Not bad at all."

We fell into a comfortable silence, the gentle ticking of the clock and the distant sound of waves the only noise in the room. As I looked out the window at the moonlit coastline, I felt a sense of peace settle over me.

"Well," Ginger said, stretching lazily, "I guess retirement isn't on the cards after all."

I chuckled, feeling a yawn coming on. "Maybe not. But bedtime definitely is. It's been a long day."

As I stood up, ready to head to bed, I paused to look at Ginger. "Thank you," I said softly. "For everything."

Ginger blinked slowly, a gesture I'd learned was a cat's way of showing affection. "Don't get sappy on me now, old man. We've got mysteries to solve."

I laughed, shaking my head. "Indeed we do, my friend. Indeed we do."

As I made my way to the bedroom, leaving Ginger to curl up in his favorite spot on the windowsill, I couldn't help but smile. Life had thrown me an unexpected curveball when I moved to Oceanview Cove, but I'd come out the other side stronger, with new friends, a renewed sense of purpose, and an extraordinary feline partner.

Whatever cases lay ahead for The Oceanview Cove Investigators, I knew one thing for certain – with Ginger by my side, I was ready to face them head-on. But first, I thought as I climbed into bed, I really needed a good night's sleep.

As I drifted off to sleep, the gentle sound of waves in the distance, I smiled to myself. Who knew retirement could be so exciting?

The End
... of the first book in the series.

Jim and Ginger's Next Case

Jim and Ginger return in *"Lost Girl"* where they take on the case of a missing teenager who vanishes without a trace.

https://mybook.to/Lost_Girl

Bonus Content

Get a FREE Jim and Ginger story!

Enjoy "The Curious Case of the Creeping Hedge" – an exclusive short story not available anywhere else!

Subscribe to Arthur Pearce's newsletter today and receive:

- Your free short story
- Updates on new releases
- Special discounts and cover reveals

https://www.arthurpearce.com/newsletter

Printed in Dunstable, United Kingdom